Finding Family... and Forever?

Teresa Southwick

HARLEQUIN® SPECIAL EDITION®

Recycling programs
for this product may
not exist in your area.

ISBN-13: 978-0-373-65802-2

FINDING FAMILY...AND FOREVER?

HARLEQUIN®
www.Harlequin.com

Printed in U.S.A.

Books by Teresa Southwick

Harlequin Special Edition

Silhouette Special Edition

Silhouette Books

Silhouette Romance

Other titles by Teresa Southwick
available in ebook format.

TERESA SOUTHWICK

lives with her husband in Las Vegas, the city that reinvents itself every day. An avid fan of romance novels, she is delighted to be living out her dream of writing for Harlequin.

Chapter One

"I'm not looking for a wife."

"Thank you for clarifying, because that's not the box I checked on the nanny application."

Justin Flint, M.D., stared at the young woman sitting across the desk from him, liking the fact that Emma Robbins had a sharp, sassy sense of humor. On the other hand, that didn't change the fact that his comment was out of line.

It was just possible he was trying to discourage her because she was too pretty. He was a Beverly Hills plastic surgeon and had relocated to Blackwater Lake, Montana, to give his almost one-year-old son a normal life. That didn't include being taken in again by a pretty face, but saying so out loud would be too weird.

"I'm sorry." He dragged his fingers through his hair. "This is going to sound egotistical, but women applying for the nanny job have been coming on to me. That's not the qualification I'm looking for in the person who's going to take care of Kyle."

"You're right. That does sound egotistical." She smiled and, if possible, was even more beautiful. "It also makes you a concerned father, which I can respect. But let me assure you, I'm not the least bit interested in anything but a job."

"Good." It *was* good but still took his ego down a peg or two. "Okay. Let's take it from the top. This interview didn't start off very well. My fault entirely. And I *assure* you that normally I behave in a completely professional way with my employees."

"I'd expect nothing less. But I can see why women flirt with you. It just has to be said that I'm not one of them."

If he were still in Beverly Hills, an agency would vet all nanny candidates, but in this small town things were different. Advertisements in the local paper and recommendations from the employees here at Mercy Medical Clinic, in addition to those of the mayor and town council, had generated half a dozen prospects. Unfortunately, the first four had clearly been more interested in batting their eyeslashes and giving him a look at their cleavage.

"All right, then." He browsed through the paperwork. "So, Miss Robbins, you're from California." That was the address she'd listed.

"Yes, Studio City. It's in the San Fernando Valley north of Los Angeles."

"Blackwater Lake is a long way from there."

She smiled. "I can see that."

He knew the Southern California neighborhood and it wasn't far from the entertainment capital of the world. With a face like hers, she could be a starlet and he'd stake his professional reputation on the fact that she'd had no work done. The flawless skin and stunning features were nothing more than excellent genes.

Emma Robbins looked as if she belonged on a movie screen. Long, shiny brown hair streaked with gold fell past her shoulders. Her eyes were brown and framed by thick lashes. But it was her mouth that mesmerized him—full, sculpted lips made for kissing, and he couldn't seem to drag his eyes away from them. *That* thought definitely hadn't been vetted by his common sense.

"So, what brought you to Montana, Miss Robbins?"

"Vacation."

"Have you ever been here before?"

"No."

"What made you decide to come here? As opposed to, say, Hawaii?" He would bet she'd turn heads in a bikini. Although right now she looked like a preppy college girl with a white collar sticking up from the neckline of her navy pullover. Tailored jeans and loafers completed the look. "I'm just trying to get to know you."

Was it his imagination or did she not quite look him in the eyes?

"This will sound corny, but one of my favorite books was set in Montana. I was between jobs and did some research. This town was advertised as the new and unspoiled Vail or Aspen. I wanted to check it out."

"So, what do you think?" he asked.

"Words can't describe how beautiful it is here," she said sincerely.

That didn't answer the question about whether or not she wanted to stay. "I need to be honest with you about my situation."

"I would appreciate that, Dr. Flint." The tone was firm, almost abrasively adamant, hinting that maybe someone hadn't been truthful with her.

Justin could relate. "I brought my current nanny with me from Beverly Hills where my medical practice was."

"Obviously there's a problem or I wouldn't be here."

"If you call hating mountains, a lake, trees and blue sky a problem, then yes."

She laughed. "I have nothing to say to that."

"The issue has more to do with missing her grown children and the fact that one of her daughters is a month away from giving birth to her first grandchild."

"That could distort your perception of the most majestic mountains ever and a lake and sky that are prettier than anything I've ever seen in my life."

He thought so, too. "The thing is, I talked her into staying until either her replacement could be found, or two weeks prebirth. Kyle hasn't known any other caregiver, and the change is going to be disruptive for him."

"How old is he?"

"Ten months."

She glanced at a photograph on his desk. "May I?"

"Please." He handed her the frame.

"He's a cutie. Just like his father." She caught herself, then met his gaze. "I swear that wasn't flirting. What I meant was, he has your eyes, and the shape of his face is all you."

He took the photo back from her and smiled at the baby, pleased she thought Kyle had inherited something good from him. Hopefully his son would have better judgment in people, specifically women people, than his old man.

"He's little and doesn't understand what's going on. I'd like the change to be as easy as possible for him."

"I can understand that." She folded her hands in her lap.

"If I decide to hire you, what assurance can you give me that you'll fulfill your obligation?"

In truth, there wasn't anything. If the sacred vows of marriage didn't stop his wife from ignoring her responsibilities, what could this stranger say to convince him? Kyle's mother had put her own interests over what was best for her son, their son. Since her death, Justin found that buying the best child care possible was the only guarantee he had.

"Dr. Flint—" She leaned toward him, earnest in her defense. "There's nothing I can say to convince you of my sincerity, but I'm well qualified. I have a degree in early childhood development and the references I provided might help ease your mind. A short-term contract would probably be best. If either of us isn't satisfied with the bargain at any time, a suitable notification period should be spelled out. Enough time for either or both of us to make other arrangements."

That seemed fair to him, but he wasn't ready to say so just yet. Instead, he asked, "What about your life in California?"

"I'm not sure what you want to know."

"Do you have family? Friends? A house to be sold or closed up?" Someone special?

Justin found himself most interested in the answer to the question he hadn't asked out loud. She was pretty. He was a guy and couldn't help noticing. She must have a boyfriend and, if not, candidates were probably lined up around the block waiting to apply for the position.

Emma sat back and crossed one slender leg over the other. "I don't have family. On top of being an only child, my father died when I was ten and Mother passed away a little less than a year ago."

"I'm sorry."

"Thank you." Her mouth pulled tight, but it looked like more than grief. "She left me the house, but I have a friend who will take care of it."

He wanted very much to know if the friend was a man, but asking wouldn't be professional. Before he could say more, there was a knock on his office door just before

Ginny Irwin, the clinic nurse, poked her head into the room. "Dr. Flint, your first afternoon appointment is here."

Since she could have relayed that information by intercom, Justin suspected she hiked upstairs to the second floor in order to get a look at the nanny applicant.

"Thanks, Ginny. I'll be right down."

"Okay." She stared curiously at the young woman across the desk from him, then backed out, closing the door behind her.

"All right," he said, "I guess we're finished."

"There's just one more thing I'd like to say." Emma picked up her purse from the floor beside her, then stood.

"What?" he asked.

"I want this job very much. And I'm very good with children."

He would check that out for himself. "All right. I have one more interview."

"Will you let me know one way or the other?"

"Yes." He stood up and felt as if he towered over her, then hated that it made him feel protective. There was something vulnerable and fragile about this woman, but getting sucked into the feeling was a bad idea. "I'll do a thorough background check and personally contact all the references you listed."

"Good. I'd expect nothing less. And I'll do the same for you."

"Oh?"

"It's a live-in position, right?"

"It is. And light housekeeping will also be required. But my primary concern is the well-being of my son. If I get called for an emergency in the middle of the night, trying to find child care could be a problem. I need someone there."

"So if I'll be living under your roof, it would be a good

idea for me to know something about you. That way, everyone feels better." She shrugged then held out her hand. "It was very nice to meet you, Dr. Flint."

Justin wrapped his fingers around hers and felt a sizzle all the way up his arm. That was enough to make him want the next job applicant to actually *be* Mary Poppins. He needed to hire someone right away. His current nanny was very close to leaving him in a real bind when she headed back to the Sunshine State.

So far, Emma Robbins was the most qualified applicant, if her references checked out. That made her the leading candidate. On the downside, he was too aware of her as a woman.

Nothing about that made him feel better.

Emma drove up the hill to Justin Flint's impressive, two-story house. After parking, she took a good look. The place was big and located in the exclusive, custom-home development of Lake View Estates. She took a deep breath and exited the car. The wraparound front porch had a white railing that opened to double front doors with etched glass. Light danced through it and was like a beacon of welcome.

"Homey," she whispered to herself. The warmth was unexpected. Maybe she'd been expecting pretentious from the renowned Beverly Hills plastic surgeon.

She walked up the three stairs and pushed the doorbell, then heard footsteps just on the other side. Bracing herself to face Justin Flint again, she wasn't prepared for the short, plump, fiftyish blonde woman who opened the door.

"I'm Sylvia Foster."

"Emma Robbins," she said, extending her hand.

"My replacement." Blue eyes twinkled good-naturedly.

"That's my hope, but I'm happy just to have a second interview." Emma hadn't expected it. The doctor had seemed distant after they'd shaken hands.

"I probably shouldn't tell you this, but he's desperate. I gave him an ultimatum and it wasn't easy. Breaks my heart to leave this baby. But…"

"He told me your first grandchild is due soon."

"A boy," Sylvia revealed, excitement sparkling in her eyes. "I'm so torn. I'll miss Kyle terribly, but my three children are in Southern California, not to mention a sister and brother. My whole family is there."

A little voice chattered unintelligible sounds behind her and she turned. On the gorgeous dark-wood entryway floor was the doctor's son, crawling toward the open door as fast as he could.

The older woman tsked, although there was no scolding in the sound. "Kyle Flint, just where do you think you're going?"

She started to bend and grab him as he scooted by her with every intention of getting outside. Emma squatted on the porch side of the low threshold and looked up at the older woman.

"It took a lot of energy for him to make a break for it. Would it be okay if he comes out just for a minute? A little reward to encourage his sense of exploration?"

"I like the way you think." Sylvia nodded and watched the baby touch the slats separating his protected world from the unknown beyond.

He sat and slapped it a few times before going on all fours again and venturing out. Turning wide eyes, his father's gray eyes, on Emma, he took her measure. Just as the doctor had done.

"Hi, cutie." She let him look, get used to her. Overwhelming him with verbal, visual and tactile stimuli could be disconcerting to the little guy.

After several moments, he crawled outside and over to her, putting a chubby hand on her thigh. Then he boosted himself to a standing position.

"He's pretty steady," she observed. "Is he walking yet?"

"Not quite," Sylvia confirmed. "He's a little hesitant to take that first step."

Emma knew how he felt. She had a family here in Blackwater Lake that she hadn't known about until just before her "mother" died. The woman had confessed to kidnapping Emma as an infant from people who lived in this town. Shock didn't begin to express how she'd felt at hearing the words, and she was still struggling to wrap her head around it all.

This trip to Montana was about her own personal exploration. She'd been in town for three and a half weeks, checked out the diner that her biological parents owned and managed. But she hadn't taken the next step of telling them who she was. Everything would change for them and there'd be no going back. She wasn't sure turning their world upside down all over again was the right thing to do. Observation showed that they'd found some sort of peace, and learning the truth might not be for the best.

The little boy slapped her jeans-clad leg and grinned as he took steps while barely holding on.

"Hey, buddy," she crooned. "You're a handsome little guy."

"A heartbreaker in training, just like his father," Sylvia said.

Emma wondered if Justin warned women away because he didn't want to break hearts. He was a doctor, after all, a healer. Or maybe he really wasn't looking for anyone because he was still grieving the wife he'd lost in a car accident. She'd checked him out on the internet and there was a lot of information on the celebrity plastic surgeon who'd given up fame and fortune due to shock and grief over losing the woman he'd loved.

An expensive silver SUV pulled up in front of the house and parked behind the little compact she'd rented at the airport nearly a hundred miles from Blackwater Lake. So the doctor was in. If this second interview went as she hoped, she'd have her car shipped from California and return the rental. The next few minutes would determine her course of action.

"Daddy's home, Kyle." Sylvia smiled at the baby and clapped her hands.

"Da—" he gurgled.

"Aren't you smart," Emma said.

She stood, gently holding the baby's upper arm to keep him from falling. Bending, she held out her hand to see if he was willing to be picked up by a stranger. He smiled and bounced, holding out his arms.

"Hey, sweetheart," she said, lifting him up and cuddling him against her. "You're a heavy boy."

Justin got out of the car and walked toward them, then up the steps. A man who looked as tired as he did had no right to still be so handsome. His short dark hair was sticking up a little, as if he'd run his fingers through it more than once that day. Piercing gray eyes grew tender when he looked at his son. In that moment he was an open book and it was as if the hidden path to his soul were exposed. He could have been a troll, but the feelings so evident on his face made him nearly irresistible.

"Sorry I'm late," he said, stopping beside Emma. "There was an emergency."

"Everything okay?" she asked, automatically swaying from side to side with the baby in her arms. Kyle had discovered the chain around her neck and the butterfly charm attached to it.

"A little girl had a run-in with broken glass." The doctor's eyes turned dark and intense when he looked at her holding his son.

"Is she okay?"

"I gave her my personal guarantee that when she's wearing her high school cheerleader uniform, no one will ever know she had stitches in her knee when she was eight."

"So you're a hero," Sylvia said.

"I wouldn't say that, but if you're passing out compliments…" He held out his arms. "Hey, buddy. Can I have a hug?"

The baby turned away and buried his face in Emma's shoulder. Not her fault, but not how a father away at work all day wanted to be greeted by the child he clearly adored.

"Hey, sweetie, want to say hi to your dad?" She wouldn't hand the boy over to his father until he was ready, or the doctor insisted.

"That's not like him," Sylvia commented. "Usually he crawls up and into your arms. I think he likes Emma. Seems very comfortable with her. Just my opinion as his primary caregiver, but you should hire her."

"And that judgment has nothing to do with the fact that you're about to leave me in the lurch."

"You're an evil man, Dr. Flint," Sylvia teased. "I don't have *enough* mother's guilt, so you feel the need to pile on more?"

"Would I do that?"

"In a heartbeat," the older woman said good-naturedly.

"Let's go inside." Dr. Flint gave no hint about whether or not he was annoyed.

Emma followed the older woman into a big entryway with a circular table holding a bouquet of fresh flowers. Twin stairways on either side led to the second story. To the left was a large formal dining room with a dark, cherrywood table and eight matching chairs. Directly to the right was the living room with a striped sofa in rust, brown and beige. Two wing chairs in a floral print with coordinating colors were arranged in front of a raised-hearth fireplace.

As they walked toward the back of the house, the little boy wiggled to get down. Emma set him on his tush, making sure he was stable before straightening. He crawled over to his father and pulled himself up before strong arms grabbed him and held him close.

"Hey, I missed you today, buddy."

He nuzzled the boy's neck and the child began to giggle. After a few moments, he pushed to get down and his father complied.

"Why don't you talk to Emma in your office," Sylvia suggested. "I'll take this little man to the kitchen and feed him."

"That would be great, Syl. Miss Robbins?"

"Lead the way," she said.

She followed him down a hall off the family room into his office where there was a large, flat-topped desk and computer. Two chairs sat in front of it and he indicated she should take one. She did, and looked around as he sat in the black leather chair behind the desk.

"This is surprisingly homey," Emma said.

"Why surprising?"

In a perfect world, Emma thought, she would have kept that observation in her head. Since it was out, she had to explain.

"I did an online search on you."

"So you checked me out." One corner of his mouth lifted.

"It's not like you weren't warned."

He didn't look at all bothered. "And?"

"You were *the* plastic surgeon to the stars. The go-to

guy for new noses, lips and—" She glanced down at her chest, which suddenly felt woefully inadequate. Then she looked up and saw the amusement in his gaze. "Other things."

"I do more than that."

"So I found out. Doctors Without Borders. Trips to Central America to work on children with cleft palates. Donating your time to Heal the Children."

"The specialty is more than just changing parts of the body a person doesn't like." He leaned forward, resting his elbows on the desk. "Most plastic surgery isn't cosmetic. It involves reconstruction. The adjective *plastic* in front of *surgery* means sculpting."

"Very interesting."

"I correct functional impairment caused by traumatic injuries, infection or disease—cancer or tumors. Sometimes a procedure is done to approximate a normal appearance. Trauma initiates sudden change, which can cause depression, make a person question who they are."

Emma had questioned who she was every day since her mother's deathbed confession about stealing her from another family when she was a baby. Plastic surgery couldn't fix her. There was no procedure that would restore what she or her biological family had lost.

"Is it my imagination, or did you quote all that from Wikipedia because you're the tiniest bit defensive about public perception regarding your field of expertise?"

"No. Maybe." His grin was a little sheepish, a little boyish and a whole lot of sexy. "Sorry. Since moving to Blackwater Lake, I've been reeducating the locals who want Angelina Jolie's lips or George Clooney's chin."

"Really? Men?"

"You'd be surprised."

"For the record, I think what you do is very impressive."

She held up her hand. "Again, not flirting or flattering. Just stating the truth as I see it."

He leaned back in the chair, more relaxed now. "Suddenly I feel like the one being interviewed."

"It was more like adding context to the information on the internet."

"I think that was a diplomatic way of saying that I like to talk about myself." There was laughter in his eyes, making them sparkle. Very different from the gray intensity that reminded her of a storm.

"You said it." She liked that he could make fun of himself.

"Speaking of interviews... Why are you surprised my house is homey?"

Too much to hope he'd been distracted enough not to remember that comment. She took a deep breath. "You made a lot of money doing what you did in Beverly Hills. I just figured your home would be chrome, glass, electronic gizmos, sculptures and art that cost the equivalent of a small country's gross national product."

His mouth pulled tight for a moment. "That was then, this is Montana. I wanted a change."

"Because of losing your wife?" Emma winced as the words came out of her mouth. She could kiss this job goodbye. If she ever faced her biological mother, one of the things she wanted to know was which side of the family to blame for this chronic foot-in-mouth problem. "Sorry. That's none of my business. You're supposed to be asking the questions."

"I am, but you touched on something important. Kyle will never know his mother, and whoever looks after him will be dealing with that issue as he gets older."

"Of course. You'll want to keep her memory alive."

"For my son."

For you, too, she wanted to say, but the sadness in his eyes stopped her. Obviously it hurt to talk about the woman. He'd probably moved here because it was too painful to live in the house and city he'd shared with the wife he loved. He'd run from his own memories but wanted to make sure his son knew about his mother.

She could relate to that. The only mother Emma had ever known wasn't really her mother and she knew next to nothing about her real family. From her perspective, information about a parent was priceless.

She'd brought up the topic but sensed he wanted to change it. "Your son is a charmer."

"He's got me wrapped around his finger." The shadows lifted from his face, leaving a tender expression.

"I can see why. So good-natured." Her cheeks grew warm remembering her own words about the boy being as handsome as the father. It was true, but she still wished to have the comment back.

"He seemed to take to you." Those eyes zeroed in on her and turned darker, more observant. "Something I needed to know. Which is why I wanted to do the second interview here at the house in Kyle's environment."

"I understand."

He nodded. "Your background check didn't turn up anything. I talked to your previous employers, who all said I'd be crazy not to hire you."

"I'm glad to hear that."

"In fact, one woman I talked to said you were personally responsible for her decision to quit her job and be a stay-at-home mother."

Emma remembered. "Carly Carrington. But her choice wasn't because I didn't do my job."

"She was very clear about that. It was about how much

you enjoyed her baby and she was jealous. Unwilling to miss any more of her child's life."

"I lost the position, but her child got the most important thing. Her mom."

"She told me you said that. So my decision all came down to chemistry."

She wasn't worried about bonding with the baby, but it was decidedly inconvenient that she was attracted to the father. Her life was way too complicated to deal with something like that even if he was interested, which clearly he wasn't. She should turn down this job right now, but the fact was, the doctor needed a nanny and she needed a job.

"I get the feeling that you've made up your mind."

He nodded. "I'm told that kids have a highly reactive blarney meter and can spot a phony a mile away. Like I said, Kyle warmed to you really fast."

"I thought so, too. And the feeling is mutual."

"That was obvious, too." He stood and walked around the desk, half sitting on the corner beside her. "So, when can you start?"

"Right away." It probably wouldn't be appropriate or professional to pump her arm in triumph, so she sat demurely with her hands folded in her lap.

"Good." He thought for a moment. "Sylvia is going back to California in two weeks. I'd like you to work with her until she leaves. Transition Kyle."

"He'll feel the change, but it will be more gradual that way," she agreed. "I appreciate this opportunity, Dr.—"

"Call me Justin."

"Okay." It was a strong name and suited him.

"I've had a short-term contract drawn up with the stipulations that we discussed in the first interview." He took a paper from his desk. "Look it over and if you're okay with everything, sign at the bottom, Emma."

It felt as if he was testing the sound of her name on his tongue, and for some reason that started tingles skipping up her spine. But she managed to read the words and signed with the pen he'd handed her.

"Welcome aboard, Emma."

"Thank you."

She wasn't sure that this opportunity was a sign of how to proceed with her own personal predicament, but it bought her time to figure everything out. She was very good at her job and he was lucky to get her, but that didn't ease her conflict. After finding out she wasn't who she'd thought, absolute truth took on a whole new meaning for her. Now she felt guilty for not confessing to Justin why she was really here in Blackwater Lake, but that wasn't an option.

What man in his right mind would hire a nanny whose whole life was a lie?

Chapter Two

Two weeks later, Sylvia was gone and Justin had just spent the first night alone with Emma. Well, not *alone,* he corrected, although it was an interesting and unforeseen way to think about her, especially since he'd never thought about his former nanny that way. Like every other morning, the smell of coffee drifted to him, but this didn't feel like just another day.

He looked in the bathroom mirror, still a little steamy from his morning shower, and applied shaving cream to his cheeks and jaw. An electric razor would be faster, but didn't do as precise a job.

The master suite was downstairs and there were five more bedrooms on the second floor along with a big open playroom area the size of the three-car garage. Emma had the room next to Kyle's with a shared bathroom between them. Sylvia would be missed, but from a father's perspective, the new nanny had been well oriented to his son's routine and she interacted with him naturally. He seemed to like her.

Justin liked her, too, in a way that was potentially prob-lematic.

After shaving and combing his hair, he dressed in jeans and a long-sleeved cotton shirt for work at Mercy Medical Clinic. There were no surgeries scheduled for today, but in the case of an emergency, he had scrubs in the office. When he was ready, he walked upstairs to spend as much time as possible with his son before leaving for the day.

At the top of the stairs he heard Emma's voice and Kyle's chattering. The nursery door was open the way it always was in the morning, so he walked in as he always did. But however much the scene was routine and famil-iar, everything felt different.

The baby was on the changing table with a clean diaper already in place. Emma had him in an undershirt and was in the process of sliding his arms into a one-piece terry-cloth romper. Her back was to him and she didn't know he was there yet.

"Hey, big boy," she crooned. "Did you have a good sleep?"

The baby was holding an orange-and-yellow plastic toy car and he clapped it against his other hand as he babbled his response.

"I'm so glad to hear it. You look well rested and I didn't hear a peep. I was listening and I'm right there if you need me. Just say, 'Hey, Em, some help here.'"

Justin moved a little farther into the room, but quietly. Not to nanny-cam her, just reluctant to interrupt this quiet, happy scene. He could see her profile and knew she was smiling. His son was grinning back, proudly showing off four top and a matching number of bottom baby teeth.

"So, what's the plan for today, Mr. Kyle? Are you going to help with laundry? Maybe the house cleaning? I know. How about you dust the toys in your basket? That would be a big help." She put a firm hand on his belly to keep him from rolling off as he unexpectedly squirmed toward her. "Not so fast. And just where do you think you're going, mister? It was a good try. Points for that. But we're not quite finished here."

She encircled his chubby leg in her fingers then bent slightly and kissed the bottom of his foot. He started to giggle and there was a smile in her voice when she said, "Are you ticklish?"

This time the smooch on his foot was accompanied by a loud smacking noise and Kyle laughed, a consuming sound that came from deep inside. Emma laughed, too, and repeated the action several more times, eliciting the same happy response.

Justin smiled at their play and would challenge anyone to keep a straight face under the same circumstances. A baby's laughter could enthrall a room full of adults. That was just a given and didn't explain his own feelings about the woman making his son laugh.

Something weird curled and tightened in Justin's gut and made this morning different from every other morning since he'd moved to Blackwater Lake. It was nothing like the other mornings he'd come upstairs to see the nanny caring for his son. But Sylvia was the grandmotherly type and Emma wasn't. That changed everything.

The sweet sound of her amusement mingling with his son's mesmerized him, and her fresh, wholesome beauty made it hard to turn away. In her jeans and soft powder-blue sweater, she was also dressed for work but on her it didn't look like work. Until yesterday, Sylvia had been there to blunt this reaction, and now all he could do was hope it would go away. Unfortunately, if anything, he felt it more sharply now that they were the only two adults in the house.

Speaking of adults, it was time to start acting like the one in charge. He moved close enough for their arms to brush and the smell of her to drift inside him. "Hey, there, you two."

Emma glanced up and smiled. "Good morning."

"Hey, buddy." He leaned down and kissed his son on the forehead. The boy babbled and held out his car. "I see. Did you sleep okay?"

The answer in baby talk sounded very much as if he were carrying on a conversation. Justin knew the chatter was the beginning of speech and his son was right on target developmentally. Absolutely normal. His goal was to maintain the average and ordinary, but the fact that his son would never have a mother already changed the usual domestic dynamic, and that bothered him. His job was all about fixing and there was nothing he could do to make this right for his son.

The child held out his arms to be picked up and Justin said, "Just a minute, buddy. You have to get dressed first."

"My fault," Emma said. "I got sidetracked. He's just too much fun to play with. I don't want you to be late because I didn't stick to the schedule."

"No problem. I'd much rather he's happy. That's the number-one priority."

She nodded then quickly and efficiently grabbed one foot at a time and slid each one into the legs of the outfit. "I'll put clothes on him later, but this is more comfortable for now."

"Sounds practical to me." When she finished, he picked up the baby and hugged him close, loving the smell of fresh-scented soap and little boy. He nuzzled the small neck until the child squealed with laughter. "I'll carry him downstairs."

"Okay. I'll get breakfast going. The coffee is ready."

She stopped in the doorway. "Is there anything special you'd like?"

You.

The thought popped unexpectedly into his mind with such intensity that it startled him. He swallowed once because his mouth was dry, then said, "Surprise me."

"Okay."

Mission accomplished, he thought, before she'd even had a chance to get downstairs. He looked into his son's gray eyes and smiled ruefully. "So, this is the new normal, kid. We just have to get used to it."

And by "we," he meant himself.

He settled the baby on his forearm and carried him downstairs and into the kitchen. There was a steaming mug of coffee sitting on the long, beige-and-black granite beside the pot.

That was something Sylvia had never done for him.

"Thanks," he said, grabbing it with his free hand.

"You're welcome." She glanced up from the bowl of raw eggs she was stirring with a wire whisk. "I'll put Kyle in his high chair."

"That's all right. I've got him and your hands are full."

The chair was set up beside the oak table in the kitchen nook that had a spectacular view of Blackwater Lake below. It was one of the things he liked best about this house. He put his mug down and settled his son, then belted him in before adjusting the tray for comfort. On the table beside it was a plastic dish of dry cereal and he set it in front of the little guy, who eagerly dug in. This was the established routine that he'd learned worked best. Keep Kyle happy so Justin could get breakfast in before work. After he left, Emma would feed him other appropriate nutritional stuff to balance his diet.

Right now she was scrambling eggs in a pan and folded

in sliced mushrooms, tomatoes and grated cheese. There was a blueberry muffin sitting by his plate. Obviously she'd been downstairs already to prepare everything before Kyle was awake.

"You're very organized," he commented. "Did you get up before God to do this?"

She looked over her shoulder and smiled. "Almost. It doesn't take long without interruptions. And this morning your son slept like a baby and made me look good."

"I just want to say that grabbing breakfast on the way to work is never a problem if he needs anything. The schedule is flexible."

"Understood," she said. "But there's always a contingency plan so you shouldn't have to."

"Like this tantalizing muffin on the table?"

"Exactly. I hope you like it."

He lifted the small plate and sniffed. "Smells good."

"I baked them yesterday afternoon while Kyle was napping."

"From scratch?"

"Yes." She used a spatula to lift the eggs onto a plate and brought it to him. "I hope this passes the taste test, too."

He sat beside his son's high chair and cut the muffin in half. Although there was butter on the table, the cakey inside was so moist he didn't think it would need any. The bite he took told him he was right. In silence, he chewed and savored the sweet, moist flavor.

Emma hovered close, waiting. "Okay. I can't stand it. Silence makes me nervous. If you hate it I need to know. I prefer honesty."

"Hate it?" He looked at her. "This is quite possibly the best blueberry muffin I've ever had, and I can't believe you didn't use a mix."

"I wouldn't lie." Her smile slipped and a sort of bruised look slid into her eyes.

Again he thought that something or someone had made the truth very important to her. "I was teasing, Emma. This is so good that if you wanted another career as a pastry chef I'd lose a very good nanny."

"I'm glad you like it." She smiled. "Hopefully, the eggs will hold up to the same scrutiny."

"I'm sure they will." He could already tell by the smell that they'd be delicious.

"Sylvia gave me lots of pointers and I took notes about your preferences. And what Kyle currently likes best. She also made sure I have her cell number and email address in case there are any questions. I'm doing my best to make the transition as seamless as possible."

"Mission accomplished."

So far she was superbly fulfilling all the objectives for which she'd been hired. His son was happy. Her cooking was really good. It wasn't her fault that the changeover could have been more seamless if she looked like Mrs. Doubtfire. If not for his blasted fascination with her, she'd be the perfect nanny.

But he'd learned the hard way that there was no such thing as the perfect woman.

Justin would be home any minute and Emma was carrying Kyle around the kitchen on her hip because it was the time of day when he was too fussy to play independently. He just wanted to be held and nothing would distract him.

"I don't mind telling you that I'm a little nervous about this first dinner on my own with you and your daddy."

Kyle looked at her then rubbed his eyes, a sure sign he was nearly at the end of his rope.

"I know, sweetie. Even after a good long nap, a busy

boy like you is just plain tired." She hugged him a little closer and her heart melted a little more at the way he burrowed against her. "The thing is, my man, your dad hasn't seen you all day and he works pretty hard. All for you, although you should never feel guilty about it. If you could hang in a little longer so he can spend some quality time with you before your bedtime, that would be pretty awesome. Okay?"

He grinned a gooey, wet grin, then babbled two syllables that sounded suspiciously like, "Okay."

Emma glanced around the kitchen and ticked things off the list in her mind. The chicken was in the Crock-Pot, a recipe that included vegetables and potatoes all together. She didn't want to tackle anything too time-consuming and labor-intensive in the final prep stages. With the little guy constantly on the move, it was a scenario with disaster written all over it.

The table was set for one adult and the high chair was ready for one baby. While Sylvia was there, they'd all eaten together, but without the older woman's presence Emma was concerned that it would feel too intimate. Justin Flint wasn't her first employer, but he was the only single dad she'd ever worked for and the dynamic was awkward. At least for her.

She found him charming and attractive and under different circumstances would probably have flirted, even though she'd sworn off men. Discovering that your fiancé was a cheating weasel tended to make a girl do that. The thing was, she wanted to flirt with Justin, but that was completely unprofessional. It was a constant strain to suppress the natural inclination.

Every time he was in the room, butterflies swarmed in her stomach. She was clumsy and tongue-tied. As if that wasn't bad enough, she was also a big fat fraud. Even though her mission in Blackwater Lake was delicate and intensely personal, it seemed wrong not to give Justin all that information before he'd made the decision to hire her. She would do her very best for this child and hope Justin wouldn't regret his decision. This job was vital in order to buy her time to decide how to handle her private situation.

The front door opened and closed, telling her that the employer she'd just been thinking about was here. A small twist of anticipation registered before she could shut it down.

She smiled at Kyle. "Your daddy's home."

"Da— Da—" He bounced in her arms and squirmed to get down.

Emma set him on the floor and instantly he got on all fours and crawled out of the kitchen as fast as he could go. She followed, not to intrude on a private father-son moment, but to make sure he made it to the safety of his dad's strong arms. Getting sidetracked on the way by something potentially harmful was always a possibility. She wouldn't let him out of her sight until she knew this house and all its baby hazards like the back of her hand. Assuming, of course, that she was here long enough to know it that well.

"Hey, buddy." In the entryway Justin had set his laptop case on the table, then grabbed up his son for a hug and kiss. "How are you?"

He lifted the baby high over his head in those strong arms she'd just been thinking about. Emma knew Kyle was sturdy and solid and holding him up like that took a lot of strength. Justin made it look easy. And the obvious love he had for his son would soften a heart harder than hers.

He settled the boy on his forearm and smiled at her. "Hi."

Some part of her brain was still functioning and she came up with a brilliant response to his greeting. "Hi."

"Something smells good."

"Chicken, potatoes, vegetables. All in the Crock-Pot." She folded her arms over her chest, an instinctively protective gesture. "It's not fancy but should taste good."

"Best offer I've had all day. I'm starved."

Emma wasn't sure, but she thought he was looking at her mouth when he said that. And there was something compelling and intense in his eyes, but probably that was just her imagination.

"It will be ready as soon as I thicken the juice for a gravy."

"Lead the way. I'll bring this guy."

Emma was more than a little self-conscious as he followed her to the kitchen. She shouldn't be; she was just the nanny. She'd started new jobs before and knew that this wasn't the usual new-job nerves. Doing her best to ignore the feeling, she headed for the Crock-Pot sitting beside the cooktop.

Behind her he said, "There's only one plate on the table."

She finished putting meat and vegetables in small casserole dishes on a warming tray then glanced at him. "I thought you'd like alone time with Kyle."

"And are you planning to eat?"

"Of course."

"When and where?" he persisted.

"Upstairs. In my room."

His eyes narrowed. "Except on her day off, Sylvia had dinner with us every night."

"I know. But…" There was no way to put this into words that he would understand. In her interview, he'd been straightforward about the fact that he wasn't looking for anything other than a nanny. To adequately explain why she wouldn't eat dinner with him, she would have to confess her attraction. Other than throwing herself at him, that was probably the fastest way to lose this job.

Justin was staring at her. "It just feels wrong to me for you to segregate yourself. Too *Upstairs, Downstairs*." He shook his head. "Or like you're an orphan in a Charles Dickens book."

That was ironic. Not only *wasn't* she an orphan, she had more family than she knew what to do with.

He settled Kyle in the high chair then met her gaze. "Emma, I'd like you to have dinner with us."

"Is that an order?"

"Of course not. It just feels…" He shrugged, as if he didn't know how to put it into words either. "I'm trying to maintain as much family atmosphere as possible for Kyle."

"I understand." And she did. "Thank you."

"I'll set another place at the table," he said.

"Okay. Thanks."

She felt pleased yet awkward at the same time. And guilty that this extraordinarily nice man didn't know the whole truth. A few minutes later the two of them were sitting in their respective places at a right angle to each other with Kyle in the middle. Emma cut chicken, cooked carrots and potato into pieces big enough for the baby to pick up with his chubby fingers but small enough so that he wouldn't choke.

Justin filled his own plate and took a bite of meat. "This is as good as it smells."

"I'm glad." She spooned some of everything for herself and tasted a little bit of each, satisfied that it was all right. "It should fill you up."

"A hearty meal for a cold night." He glanced at his son, who was busy with his food, part eating part playing. "Kyle approves, too."

"Do you like chicken salad?"

"Yeah." He met her gaze. "Why?"

"I can make some with the leftovers. A little celery, cucumber. Maybe dill pickle chopped up?"

"Sounds good to me."

She knew from her two weeks of orientation with Sylvia that he sometimes took lunch with him to Mercy Medical Clinic. "I can make a sandwich for you if you'd like. Maybe a piece of fruit and macaroni salad."

"If it's not too much trouble, that would be great."

"I'm happy to do it." Emma was being well paid for her work, but it didn't feel like work because she wanted to please him. That's what bothered her the most.

Justin chewed a carrot then glanced at his son, who had little orange pieces of vegetable all over his face. "Tell me what he did today."

"He was an angel."

"Don't sugarcoat it. What was this scoundrel really up to?"

She smiled. "It's the absolute truth. He's practically perfect. And by that I mean perfectly normal for his age."

"What you're diplomatically telling me is that my son got into everything. Or tried."

"Yes, he did."

"So, how is that perfect?"

"It's exactly what he should be doing. Natural curiosity in a child is completely appropriate. Exploring his environment is his job." She smiled. "And he's really good at it."

"He kept you running?"

She nodded. "It's my job to make his surroundings secure. If I had a chore to do, I set up an area with a safe zone for him. And he loves to help. Folding towels, for instance. Did you know he loves the laundry basket?"

"I didn't." He tousled the boy's downy, light brown hair.

"Way to go, buddy." In answer, Kyle slapped the high-chair tray, splattering food.

"And anything that needed doing in a nonsafe zone waited until he was down for a nap." She sounded like a walking baby textbook, but it was important that he know how his son was being cared for. "He took a long one this afternoon, but now he looks tired to me. I have a feeling he's growing."

"What makes you think so?"

"Look at the way he's eating."

Justin laughed ruefully. "It's really hard to judge how much is actually going in."

"I gave him quite a bit and he's not wearing that much of it," she said, smiling at the grubby boy. "Do you like it, Kyle?" He shook his head but was grinning. "Silly."

"That's my boy."

"He also needs more sleep, which is an indication of a growth spurt."

"Good to know."

There was silence for several moments and to fill it she said, "How was your day?"

"Calm. Routine. On schedule." He wiped his mouth on a napkin. "Mostly surgery follow-up appointments and I'm happy to report all the patients followed doctor's orders and are progressing well. Then there were consultations for elective surgical procedures. Stuff like that."

"Nothing out of the ordinary? No emergencies?"

"No. It's a good day when that happens."

"I'm glad."

Uneventful *was* a good thing. Her life had been just the opposite of that lately. And this dinner was no exception. On the surface it was a peaceful, seemingly normal meal, but she couldn't help feeling as if talking about their respective days blurred the line between employer and employee.

Maybe the mountain air was messing with her mind. Lack of oxygen was doing a number on her head. What felt like thirty seconds ago, she'd broken her engagement to a man she'd learned was a liar and cheat. Now here she was thinking flirty thoughts about the employer who signed her paycheck and praying she didn't forget herself and kiss him goodbye as he went off to work.

The right thing would be to confess to him the whole truth, then offer her resignation, but she couldn't. Not yet. For the time being she had to keep her secret.

Chapter Three

"Our first trip to the grocery store, little man."

Not surprisingly, Emma heard no verbal response from the rear seat where Kyle was happily staring out the window of her midsize SUV. It had arrived from California, and Justin had approved the safety factor. He'd installed the baby's car seat himself, even though all child-related equipment was in her sphere of expertise.

It was kind of endearing how seriously Dr. Flint took his responsibilities as a father. That was another check mark in her employer's "pro" column. Not that she was actively looking for "cons," but it would help. In the few days since she'd become the solo nanny, her attraction to him hadn't subsided.

She drove down Main Street and turned left into the parking lot of the town's biggest market, appropriately named The Grocery Store. There were smaller stores for gourmet olive oil, coffee, health foods and specialty items, but this was where Sylvia had suggested she go for the bulk of the shopping. There weren't too many cars here on this weekday morning and that suited Emma just fine.

She parked and turned off the ignition, then grabbed her purse and the diaper bag before exiting. After rounding the vehicle, she opened the rear passenger door and released the straps on the car seat to lift Kyle out. Propping him on her hip, she walked to the automatic doors with neat rows of shopping carts beside them. She released one then fished the cheerful animal-print seat liner out of the diaper bag and arranged it before lifting the baby in.

"Can't be too careful," she told him. "There are enough germs in the world that I can't protect you from, but this I can do." She smiled at him and he grinned in response.

"You're in a good mood, big guy." His answer was an unintelligible sound that she liked to think of as affirmative.

Pushing the cart, she walked into the store and scanned the layout, preferring to pick up boxed and nonperishable items first. After that, she'd get things like milk and the cream Justin liked in his coffee.

She watched Kyle scratch at a giraffe on the seat cover. "You seem like a naturally cheerful little soul to me. Did you get that disposition from your daddy?"

She walked down the baby-products aisle and grabbed baby wipes and the largest package of disposable diapers, which she set on the very bottom of the cart. After that, she bypassed cleaning products and headed for cereal and canned goods. There was no one around and she chattered away to her little charge as she picked up canned tomatoes for a batch of marinara and some enchilada sauce for a recipe Justin liked.

"So far, your dad seems like a pretty agreeable sort, too. I sure hope so, because if he ever finds out the whole truth, I could be in trouble."

Rounding the corner to turn down the next aisle, Emma was trying to take in everything around her and not paying attention to where she was going. In her peripheral vision she saw another shopper. Just in time to avoid a cart collision, she pulled up short and automatically apologized. Then she got a good look at the woman she'd almost hit and her heart stopped, skipped once then started to pound. There were very few shoppers in this store and of all the people to run in to...

She was face-to-face with Michelle Crawford, her biological mother.

"I'm really sorry," she mumbled. "Not watching where I was going."

"No harm done. You've got pretty good reflexes."

Emma's mind was racing as fast as her heart. Questions without answers rattled around in her head. Should she say something about their connection? In a place as public as a grocery store? Was there a perfect place to drop the bombshell of who she really was? Getting away as fast as possible seemed like the very best idea.

She started to push her cart past the other woman. "Have a nice day."

"Hello, Kyle. How are you?"

Emma looked at the baby, who was staring uncertainly, as if he sensed her tension. "How do you know him?"

"The doctor brings him into the diner when Sylvia has the night off." She looked more closely. "You must be the new nanny."

And so much more. "That's right."

"Welcome to Blackwater Lake. I'm Michelle Crawford."

"Emma Robbins. Nice to meet you."

Emma took the hand the other woman held out, half expecting it would be a conduit to her thoughts. She braced for an aha moment that didn't happen. It would have been too easy. She was simply a stranger, a newcomer to Blackwater Lake.

Finally she pulled herself together and met her mother's gaze. Emma was looking into brown eyes the same shade as her own. The two of them were the same height and their hair was a similar shade of brunette, although silver streaked the other woman's.

"I own the Grizzly Bear Diner. With my husband," she added. Apparently she hadn't seen Emma there. "Actually, Alan and I were co-owners with Harriet Marlow. She met a man on one of those internet dating sites and they had a phone relationship for a while because he's from Phoenix. That went well, so he came all the way to Blackwater Lake to meet her in person. They fell in love and she decided Arizona was a good place to retire. So, my husband and I bought her out. She married him and moved away."

"Wow." At least someone got their happily-ever-after.

"Listen to me. Blathering on. Is that what kids call TMI?"

Too much information. Emma hadn't thought it possible that she could laugh but she did. "No. Finding love is always good information. I guess."

"Sounds like you have a bad story."

"Could be."

So far, Michelle hadn't put her foot in her mouth, so Emma couldn't say she'd inherited the tendency there. However, she did lean toward blathering in certain situations, although the one in progress didn't appear to fall into that category because she wasn't saying much.

"Where are you from, Emma?"

"Southern California."

Should she go with the partial story she'd told Justin? The truth, even half of it, was easiest to keep straight.

But Michelle continued talking and saved her from having to respond. "Montana weather is really different from where you lived. It gets cold here in the mountains. It's

September and already heading in that direction. Are you ready for snow?"

"I guess we'll find out."

"If you need any winter-survival tips, just come over to the diner. Alan and I will be glad to help you out."

"Thanks. I wouldn't want to be a bother." Emma meant that more sincerely than this woman could possibly know.

She waved a hand, dismissing the concern. "It's no bother. You'll find people here in Blackwater Lake are really friendly. Willing to help out their neighbors."

"That's good to know." Also reassuring to learn her biological mother seemed to be a really good person.

Kyle chose that moment to join the conversation. Along with the stream of chatter, he started to wriggle in the cart, trying to pull his legs free and climb out.

"Just where do you think you're going, Mr. Kyle?" She laughed when he held out his arms. "I think that's my cue to get a move on."

"Kids do let you know..."

Emma was just starting to get comfortable, to shake off the urge to run. But Kyle came first and he was obviously getting restless. "It's time to finish up the shopping."

"You're not the only one. I'm due at the diner for the lunch rush. Alan will send out a search party if I'm late."

Because a member of his family had disappeared once? She couldn't imagine what that must have felt like.

"I've got to get this little one home for lunch and a nap."

"He seems like a good baby."

"That's an understatement. He's practically perfect."

Michelle studied her. "You seem really fond of him."

"That's what Dr. Flint pays me for."

"It's more than that." The other woman rested a palm on the handle of her basket... "The way you look at him is something a paycheck can't buy."

Emma shrugged. "I like kids."

"So do I."

"But Kyle is especially easy to like."

"I can see that."

Emma glanced at her watch and saw that it was pushing noon. "I'm sorry to keep you."

"It's all right." But the sad, wistful expression that slid into her eyes as she looked at the baby said something was *not* right. The warm friendliness from moments ago faded.

"Is something wrong?"

"Not really. No," she said firmly, as if she was working hard to make that the truth. "It was nice talking to you, Emma. I hope we'll see you in the diner."

"Maybe."

She watched the other woman walk away and knew this perfect, happy baby had been a reminder of what was taken from her. At first, she'd been bubbly and outgoing, then they started talking about Kyle. That had made her withdraw. Apparently, she'd learned to cope with the loss and had come to terms with it.

Seeing the change convinced Emma that she was right to keep her identity to herself. She was a grown-up now and couldn't give the woman back the baby girl she used to be. Shaking up Michelle Crawford's world all over again just didn't seem like the right thing to do.

Justin walked up his front steps and realized he was whistling. He didn't whistle; he'd never whistled. And it had nothing to do with a radio tune looping in his head because he'd been listening to news on the way home from the clinic. He realized it was a symptom of a condition he hadn't experienced for a long time. It was called happiness.

Part of the reason was seeing his son content. Growing and thriving in this place that couldn't be more different from Beverly Hills. The other part was about the woman who was making sure his son was happy.

Emma Robbins.

Just thinking her name produced an image of her in his mind, and the vision was enough to make his senses quiver with anticipation. If she had a flaw, he couldn't see it. Not only was she easy on the eyes, she took care of Kyle as if he were her own. And she was a great cook. Her inclusion into the household had been seamless.

He jogged up the steps to the front door and unlocked it, then stepped inside. "I'm home."

Justin felt an irrational impulse to add "honey." Maybe it was time for a mental health professional to join the staff at Mercy Medical Clinic. A shrink would have a field day with him. Diagnosis: unreasonable romantic feelings where there weren't any because he was obsessed with having an intensely loving and respectful relationship like the one his parents had enjoyed.

His first marriage had been a failure, which meant he'd already screwed up any chance of following in his mom and dad's footsteps. That wasn't a failure he wanted to repeat, but it was hard to remember why when he looked at Emma's mouth.

"We're in the kitchen," she called out.

"On my way."

Just the sound of her voice, which was two parts silk and one part gravel, made him want to start whistling again. He held back as he walked to his home office and put his laptop on the desk. Then he joined them at the dinner table where Emma sat beside Kyle, who was in the high chair.

"Daddy's home," she said to the boy.

"Da—" He didn't look up, too deep in concentration. With tiny thumb and forefinger he picked up a pea and put it in his mouth.

Emma clapped her hands at the accomplishment. "Good job."

The boy grinned at her praise, and then went after a small piece of cooked carrot.

"I tried to hold off his dinner until you got home," she explained. "But he was just too hungry."

"No problem." The room was filled with tantalizing smells that made him realize Kyle wasn't the only hungry guy in the family. "What's for dinner?"

"Rigatoni and meatballs. Salad. Now that you're here, I'll cook the pasta."

"Sounds good. I'll just visit with this guy while you do that."

Her only response was a smile that did amazing things to her mouth. One glance was like touching a hot stove and he pulled back, turning his attention to the neutral subject of peas and carrots.

Justin put a few on the plastic tray. "Here you go, buddy."

"Da—Da—" After slapping both small hands on the vegetables, Kyle rubbed the mushed goo into his hair and over his face.

Justin laughed and said, "Code green emergency."

Standing at the stove in front of a pot steaming with simmering pasta and another bubbling with marinara and meatballs, Emma glanced over her shoulder. "That means he likes them."

"I'll have to take your word for that because wearing food seems counterproductive to the goal."

"Just wait and see how much he likes my rigatoni and red sauce."

Justin groaned. "Dear God—"

"Prayer is pointless. Straight upstairs to the bath for him. It's why messy meals are at night."

"A good plan."

"I try."

She looked over her shoulder to satisfy herself that all was well before sliding her hands into oven mitts. After lifting the boiling pot of pasta, she poured the contents into a colander in the sink and let it drain.

Five minutes later the two of them were eating salad and Kyle was popping pieces of rigatoni into his mouth and smacking his lips.

"I know what you mean, kid. This is really good, Emma."

"I'm glad you like it."

For the first time, Justin had a chance to study her. There were shadows in her eyes obscuring the sparkle that he'd come to expect.

"Is everything all right?" he asked.

"Yes." She looked up quickly, but her gaze didn't quite meet his. "Why?"

"Just checking." He cut a meatball and forked half into his mouth. After chewing and swallowing, he asked, "What did you guys do today?"

"Grocery shopping." Her mouth pulled tight for a second, then she moved lettuce around her plate without eating any.

He wasn't imagining the tension. "How did that go?"

"Fine."

Obviously she and Kyle were home safe and sound. The household supplies were replenished, all of which indicated a successful shopping experience. But he couldn't shake the feeling that something had happened. Justin wanted to know what, but since it didn't appear to have any connection to his son, he had no right to grill her like raw hamburger. For all he knew, it could be about her love life.

The background check hadn't turned up a significant other, although that didn't mean there wasn't one. He didn't like the idea of Emma being in love, but that had nothing to do with Kyle and everything to do with a feeling he'd had little experience with.

Jealousy. He wasn't proud of it, but there was no denying the truth.

Maybe he'd ask a few questions, after all. "So what did you think of Blackwater Lake's premier grocery store?"

The expression on her face turned wry. "It's the only grocery store. And it seemed fine."

"Kyle wasn't a problem?"

"Not at all." She cut a rigatoni and speared half with her fork but didn't eat it. "How was your day?"

This question had come up every night since she'd taken over from Sylvia, but this time it smacked of changing the subject. There was no subtle way to push harder, so he decided to back off. But he couldn't resist giving her a taste of her own medicine.

"My day was fine," he said.

"I'm glad."

After that, they made small talk while he finished dinner. She ate very little, mostly pushing her food around the plate. When Kyle got grouchy and restless, she jumped at the chance to take him upstairs for a bath.

"I'll clean up the kitchen," he said.

"No, leave it for me."

Emma scooped Kyle out of the high chair and held him against her, oblivious to the red sauce and smashed peas that got all over her shirt. He couldn't help comparing her to the baby's mother, who wouldn't touch her own child if he was less than immaculate.

"You do enough," he insisted. "I don't mind squaring things away here."

She looked as if she wanted to protest but nodded and carried Kyle out of the kitchen and upstairs.

Justin stowed the leftovers, rinsed plates and utensils then scrubbed the pots. The busywork occupied his hands, but his mind raced. He thought about the employees at the clinic, body language and bad mood indicating when someone was dealing with a personal problem. It never occurred to him to get involved, but none of the clinic staff lived under his roof and cared for the child he loved more than anything in the world.

He heard sounds from upstairs—splashing, laughter and baby chatter. There was clinic paperwork to do, but he suddenly felt as if he were on the outside looking in. After drying his hands, he went upstairs and found the two of them in the bathroom where water was draining out of the tub.

Emma covered her front with a thick terry-cloth towel then lifted the baby out of the tub and wrapped him up. She carried him to the nursery then diapered him as quickly as possible. All the red-and-green smears were gone, although she still sported them on her clothes. But Kyle was now a clean boy with neatly combed hair.

"That was quick," Justin said.

"He's tired." With quick efficiency, she put the baby in a small, soft blue one-piece sleeper and picked him up. Then she headed for the glider chair in the corner beside the crib. "It was a busy day. You can see the signs when he's had it and is ready to go to sleep."

"I'll rock him tonight. You take a break."

"That's not necessary—"

"I insist. Kyle had a busy day, which means yours was even more tiring. Just take some time and relax."

She tilted her head and studied him. "Are you sure?"

"Positive."

"Okay." She walked over and started to hand the baby to Justin, but he let out a wail and clung to her, curling against her with his face buried in her neck. "I'm sorry. Do you want to just grab him?"

"No." He moved close and put his hand on the small back. "It's okay, buddy. I know you're tired."

And his son wasn't the only one. That was as good an explanation as any for his own intense reaction to the warmth of Emma's skin, the scent of her that twisted his senses into a knot of need. The only good thing was that it pushed jealousy out of the number-one position.

"Kyle?" Emma crooned softly. "Daddy's here. Don't you want some man time with him?"

As if he understood, the baby lifted his head and held out his arms. Justin took him and said, "That's my guy. We're just going to sit in the glider and have a little chat. I'll tell you a story. I get the feeling that reading would be a bad idea tonight."

"I think you're right about that." Emma headed for the door. "You're sure you don't mind?"

"Yeah, I'm sure. I don't do this enough."

The baby clinging to her was proof. On the one hand, he was glad Kyle had bonded with her so completely. The flip side of that was that Justin didn't have the same connection. It was good to have a reminder that he needed to spend more quality time with his son.

Just before walking out of the room, Emma stopped. "Justin?"

"Hmm?" He sat in the chair and settled the baby to his chest, then met her gaze.

"Would you mind if I borrowed your computer in the office? My laptop is acting squirrelly."

"Of course." He smiled and started the chair gliding back and forth. Almost instantly Kyle relaxed into him. "And, for the record, squirrelly is not an official technological term."

The corners of her full lips turned up. "And there's a good reason for that. I don't speak fluent tech."

"Ah."

"Thanks."

Her words were light and teasing but didn't match the expression on her face. It could only be described as tense, distracted. Before he could study her more, she was gone.

He rubbed his hand over his son's back and moved slowly, lulling him to sleep. "What's going on with your nanny, Kyle? You obviously are attached to her and I'm glad about that, but there's something up with her. The good news is that she's not very good at hiding her feelings."

In a matter of minutes, his baby boy was sound asleep. He waited a little longer, moving gently to make sure before putting him down in the crib. A short time later, that was accomplished without a peep, and Justin covered him with a baby blanket, then softly kissed the tiny forehead.

"I love you, buddy." For a few moments he stood over his son, watching the rhythmic rise and fall of the little chest, savoring the peace of knowing his child was safe and happy.

He picked up the baby monitor and soundlessly left the room, going downstairs. Emma was nowhere in sight and he remembered she was using his home computer. After pouring himself a cup of coffee, he walked down the hall and into his office. Emma's back was to him as she looked at the computer monitor and he moved closer to the desk.

On the screen in big, bold letters was a newspaper headline that read, "KIDNAPPED! BABY GIRL DISAPPEARS. STOLEN FROM A BLACKWATER LAKE FAMILY."

The date on the article was about twenty-eight years before, and Emma was completely engrossed in reading the information. She hadn't heard him approach and never looked up.

This appeared to be a private thing, but Justin didn't give a flying fig if he was overstepping. She had some explaining to do and it was going to happen now.

"Interesting stuff," he said.

She jumped, then pressed her hand to her chest and swiveled the chair around to look at him. "Good gracious. You startled me."

"Startling pretty well describes it. And I'm talking about what you're reading on the computer." The look on her face told him that she was hiding something. "What's going on, Emma?"

"If you want to look for another nanny, I completely understand. And that would probably be best since I lied to you."

Uh-oh. Just a while ago he'd thought that if she had a flaw he couldn't see it. Well, she'd just pointed one out and it was a beaut. What could possibly be so bad that Emma felt she had to keep it from him? If she'd broken the law, it would have turned up in her background check. Her record was spotless yet she'd just admitted she'd been less than honest.

Could a woman as sweet as Emma seemed to be have something in her past that was worse than his own guilty secret? No one knew how he'd really felt about the wife who died and that wasn't information he wanted to share. A problem for another day. Finding a new nanny wasn't what he wanted and he hoped her lie turned out to be a fib about the weight on her driver's license.

But he wasn't whistling now.

Chapter Four

"What lie? I can't imagine you've done anything that bad."

"Justin, I…" Emma didn't know what to say to him, how to soften what had happened to her. Then she figured there was no point in carefully picking words. Saying it straight out was the only way. "I didn't tell you the whole truth when you asked why I picked Blackwater Lake for my vacation."

"So, you didn't read a book set in Montana?"

His expression was serious, but she would swear the question was meant to lighten the mood. It seemed empathetic somehow, as if he understood or at least wanted to. But he couldn't until she explained and then she would have to accept the consequences, whatever they might be.

She realized she was sitting behind his desk and stood, rounding it to stand in front of him. She met his gaze and forced herself not to look away. "I came here to meet my biological parents."

"So your secret is that you were adopted?"

"Not exactly."

He looked at the computer monitor where the newspaper headline from the past screamed out. The incident was years old, but not to her. It was fresh and painful, complicated and confusing.

His eyes moved over the words of the article and the expression in them said he'd skimmed the contents and was making guesses. "What exactly?"

Emma's legs were trembling and she desperately wanted to rest a hip against the desk but wouldn't show weakness. This was the mess she'd made by not being completely up front with him in the beginning. It was honesty time and she'd do that standing up straight.

"I was kidnapped as a baby and raised by the woman who took me."

Shock and anger hardened his face. "And you never knew she wasn't your mother?"

"Not until recently. When she was diagnosed with cancer, the disease progressed very quickly. Just before she died, she confessed the truth and told me where I came from, where to find my biological family. They live here in Blackwater Lake."

He rested a hand on the back of one of the chairs in front of the desk. "How did she explain turning up with a baby? Not being pregnant? Weren't there questions?"

"I don't know. I was a baby." She shrugged. "My dad—the man I thought was my dad—died when I was a kid. She, my mother—" Emma shook her head. "She's not my mother, but it's hard for me to think of her any other way. What she did was wrong—"

"Yeah."

"But I never knew her as anything other than loving and kind. She was Mom to me." Emma looked away for a moment and shook her head. "I was too little to remember anything else. She was a single mom when they met and if my dad knew what she'd done and was complicit in the whole thing, he never did or said anything that made me question my family. I don't know how she explained everything. And at the end she was very weak." She shrugged helplessly. "I didn't know any different. They were my parents. She was my mother and there was never any reason to question it."

Justin dragged his fingers through his hair then met her gaze. "Would you like a glass of wine?"

She'd love one, but she never had alcohol when there was a child in her care. It might be his way of subtly preparing her to be let go. "Unless this is your way of firing me, I'm on the job and I don't drink when I am."

"Emma..." He moved closer and looked down as if he wanted to touch her. It was a disappointment when he didn't.

The yearning to burrow against him for comfort was a different kind of problem and she couldn't deal with it right now. She studied his expression, tried to guess what he was thinking. "Justin, for all you know, I could be making this up."

"But you're not."

"How do you know? I deceived you once."

"Withholding information isn't deception. The personal facts were yours to do with as you saw fit. And the thing is, I'm mostly a good judge of people. I was only really wrong once." There was a grim look in his eyes. "I don't think you're a good enough actress to not be telling the truth about this."

She was relieved that he believed her, but it still didn't mean he wanted to keep her as his son's nanny. "Don't be nice to me. I need to know where I stand."

He ignored that. "Kyle is asleep. One glass of wine won't be a problem if he needs anything. And I'm here."

Yes, he was. She was always aware of him when he was in the house. She shook her head. "I really shouldn't."

"You're shaking. It will help."

Emma looked at her trembling hands and realized he was right. She stuck them in her jeans pockets. "That sounds good. Are you sure you don't mind?"

"Consider it doctor's orders."

He held out his hand and she put hers in it, then let him lead her from the office into the kitchen. She missed the warmth and strength of his touch when he sat her at the table and moved away. But after taking advantage of his trust, this was more consideration than she deserved. While he was busy assembling glasses and opening a bottle, she stared out the window. The patio and rear yard were illuminated by perimeter lights, but darkness and shadows hid the incredible view of the lake and the mountains beyond it.

Emma felt as if she was finally moving out of the shadows that had swirled around her for months. Whatever Justin decided about her employment she would have to live with because the decision to keep this to herself had been hers alone. But for right now it was an enormous relief to talk about everything.

He set a glass of white wine in front of her, then sat down at a right angle. "I hope you like chardonnay."

"Right now you could give me balsamic vinegar and I'm not sure I could taste the difference."

"It must have been a shock to find out what happened to you."

"*Shock* is such a bland word to describe how I felt. It was so surreal, something that happens to other people, not to me."

"The fact is, we're all 'other' people. The news is full of ordinary human beings who have gone through extraordinary things. It's how one copes and moves on that matters. What did your friends say?" he asked.

"I haven't told them."

He was just taking a drink of wine and slowly lowered the glass. "No one knows?"

"My fiancé. And now you."

Again his surprise showed. "Really?"

"Yes. It didn't work out. No need for you to worry that I'll go back to him and leave you without someone to care for Kyle." She saw more questions in his eyes, but didn't feel like getting into it. "If it's all right with you, I'd rather not talk about him."

"Okay." He nodded. "But you didn't tell your other friends about this? Why?"

Emma knew what he was really asking was why she hadn't said anything to people she knew better than him. After sipping her wine, she said, "Mom died shortly after telling me, so there was a funeral to plan and it wasn't something I wanted to bring up then. A decent length of time passed and I didn't know how to start that conversation. It seemed wrong to say, You know my mother who died? She actually wasn't my mother. She stole me from another family."

"Why did she tell you?"

"I guess because confession is good for the soul. She wanted to clear her conscience before she died."

"Why didn't you come to see your biological family sooner?"

"A lot of reasons." Emma drank more wine as she gathered her thoughts, trying to figure out how to make him understand. "I was grieving the woman who'd loved and raised me. A woman I'd loved because she was good to me. Not only that, I had a job. I'd signed a contract and there was a child to take care of. And I was engaged to be married. As the days went by, I figured I'd come to terms with everything and let it go."

"What changed?"

"I found out my fiancé was cheating on me. He was one more trusted person in my life who was lying. I guess it hit a nerve."

"No kidding."

"And I've sworn off men." She almost smiled. "It was more than just being hurt. I'd recently learned my whole life was a lie and to find out he was a two-faced scumbag made me question who I am. I needed to find some truth."

"So you came to Blackwater Lake."

"Yes. My biological parents own the Grizzly Bear Diner."

"Michelle and Alan Crawford." He nodded slowly as the information sank in. "So you've met your family."

Emma chose her words carefully. "I've seen them."

"They must have been over the moon to find out their missing daughter is alive and well."

"I don't know how they'd feel about that."

His eyes narrowed. "You haven't told them?"

"Until today, I hadn't even talked to them." She took a deep breath. "I ran into Michelle Crawford at the grocery store."

"So that's why you've been preoccupied." Justin's gray eyes darkened with questions. "How did it go?"

"She's very nice. Friendly. And she'd looked sad when Kyle chattered nonstop in his sweet baby way. The encounter shook me. I couldn't get it out of my mind. I needed to see the newspaper accounts of the kidnapping again."

"But she still doesn't know?" When Emma shook her head, he said, "I'm sure you had your reasons for not telling them who you are."

"It's complicated."

"No kidding." His tone was wry.

"My mother told me where they are and how to find them." She took a big drink from her glass. "When I got here, the Grizzly Bear Diner was my first stop. Michelle and Alan were there and I watched them interacting with the customers and each other. They're—" She struggled to figure out how to say they seemed like two people who were content and working at something they enjoyed. It was hard to express, when one picture was worth a thousand words. "They seemed okay. I didn't want to change that."

"And you think finding out their daughter is alive would be a bad thing?"

"What happened to them was bad."

"Can't argue with you there." But his eyes narrowed. "Still, you said nothing?"

"There's probably no way for you to understand, but I just couldn't."

"So why didn't you go back to California?"

There was the burning question, and she didn't have an answer. "I couldn't do that, either."

"But you needed a job while you figure it all out."

It wasn't a question, but she felt he deserved an answer, anyway. "Yes, and you wouldn't have hired me if I'd told you all that."

"We'll never know." He finished the wine in his glass then met her gaze. "I'm going to give you a piece of advice, but keep in mind it's worth what you paid for it."

"Okay." She braced herself.

"My parents had the kind of marriage that everyone wants but so many don't get. They're both gone now, but every day together they taught me what love looks like. Then my son showed me how it feels, what unconditional means. I couldn't begin to imagine losing him. So, for what it's worth, you should tell the Crawfords who you are."

"You don't—"

He held up his hand to stop her. "All I'm saying is that if it were me, I'd want to know."

"That's easy for you to say."

"I know. I'm not walking in your shoes. Or theirs, either. But that's what I think."

It was so easy to stand on the outside looking in and give an opinion. But Emma needed to be sure what the right thing was because once the words were said there was no going back. So the story she should have told him in the beginning was out now and it was time to save them both an awkward conversation.

She stood. "So, I'll just go upstairs and pack my things."

"Why?"

"Because you're going to fire me. It will be uncomfortable for you to say and humiliating for me to hear since I've never been dismissed from a job before. So, I'll make this easier on both of us and just go quietly."

He put a hand on her arm when she started to move away. "Not so fast."

"But, Justin, I lied to you."

"Everything about your professional background was the absolute truth. There was no lie. It was more about not revealing personal details, which technically you're not obligated to do."

"But you know as well as I do that puts my personal life up in the air and it's not fair to you."

"What I know is that you're terrific with Kyle and I would like you to stay. If that becomes impossible, all I ask is a decent amount of notice so that I can replace you."

The knot in her belly started to unravel. "That's very generous of you."

"Actually, it's selfish."

"You say potato, I say po-tah-to." Emma wanted to argue with him but figured she shouldn't look a gift horse in the mouth. "Thank you."

He waved the words away. "I'm just sorry you had to go through what you did. If I can help in any way, please let me know."

"I appreciate that very much." More than she could even put into words.

So, the truth was out there and it felt good to come clean to Justin. She was relieved that he knew the whole truth.

That was sort of what she was doing to Michelle and Alan Crawford, but it felt different. She was in control of this information. It affected her, too, and everything would change if they knew she was their daughter. Before taking that step, she needed to know more about her family.

"The best way to get acquainted with the Crawfords is to spend time with them."

It was Saturday and Justin had shut off his laptop and stopped working on patient medical records in order to spend time with his son. This was Emma's night off and usually he took Kyle to the Grizzly Bear Diner for dinner. He'd asked Emma to come along and she was less than enthusiastic about the invitation.

He leaned back against the kitchen island and folded his arms over his chest. Studying her anxious expression, he said, "You're scared."

"That's ridiculous." The baby crawled over and pulled himself to a standing position, using her leg for leverage. She lifted him into her arms and automatically hugged him close.

"No one blames you for being scared."

Justin had been mulling over what she'd told him and as

secrets went, hers wasn't that bad. None of it was her fault. He couldn't say the same about his past. All he wanted was to forget that he hadn't been in love with his wife for a long time before she died, and they were planning to get a divorce when she'd been involved in a fatal car accident.

Like Emma's story, this was personal information that had no direct bearing on his job performance. Everyone assumed he was in mourning and it was easier not to correct that impression because he didn't want to talk about that mistake. He would never have wished her dead, but it would be a lie to say he missed her. For reasons he didn't understand, it was very important that Emma not know about all that ugliness. She wouldn't like him very much and he couldn't blame her. Hell, he didn't much like himself.

"Look, Justin—I'm not afraid to see my family." She met his gaze. "Just cautious."

Justin wanted to help resolve the situation. It was a lousy thing for Alan and Michelle, who were good people, but he hated the bruised and betrayed look in Emma's eyes. Also, she was right. Her situation was unstable and a difficult reunion with the family she'd just discovered could send her running back to California.

"Caution is good. Who would know that better than a doctor. The cornerstone of the Hippocratic Oath is to do no harm. Going to their diner on Saturday night when the place is busiest would be a careful first step. They won't even notice you, but that makes it possible to check them out from afar." Justin decided a hint of challenge wouldn't be a bad thing. "What else have you got to do on your night off? You don't have a date."

"How do you know?" There was a saucy, sassy, rebellious expression in her eyes.

"Because you've sworn off men."

Justin realized he was unreasonably pleased about that. He didn't especially like the idea of her dating. She was a beautiful woman and men would notice. *He'd* noticed and couldn't seem to stop. There wasn't anything he could do to prevent her from seeing another man. She was under no obligation to tell him what she did in her free time.

"You remembered," she said.

"Yeah."

"Too much information." Her expression was charmingly sheepish. "Although true. And you're right. I don't have plans."

That was a relief but also made him feel guilty and he wondered what she did when she wasn't caring for Kyle. Was she meeting people? Making friends? Putting down roots in Blackwater Lake? Part of him hoped so for his son's sake. For himself, he didn't need or want this attraction.

"So you're free." He met her gaze. "Then there's no reason you can't have dinner with Kyle and me. At the diner. What can it hurt?"

"Nothing, I guess."

That still wasn't enthusiastic, but he'd take it as a yes before she changed her mind. He looked at the baby. "Kyle, want to go for a ride?"

The little boy's eyes lit up and he held out his arms to Justin who took him from her. "I'll get his jacket," he told Emma. "Meet you at the front door in five."

"Okay." She started out of the room, then stopped in the doorway and said, "I lied when I said I wasn't scared. I am a little afraid. But it's not a habit. The lying part. Maybe just a little defensive."

"We'll keep that between you and me." The words made her smile and he felt the familiar tug in his gut that was all about wanting to kiss her.

Twenty minutes later, the three of them walked into the Grizzly Bear Diner. It wasn't quite six o'clock and not too crowded yet, so they were seated right away. Violet, one of the servers, brought over a high chair and Emma pulled out a disposable antiseptic wipe from a package in the diaper bag. She started cleaning the straps and tray of the chair.

"No offense," she said to the waitress.

"None taken. The other moms who come in do the same thing." The girl was blonde, blue-eyed and probably in her late teens. She looked at the three of them. "You guys are a really beautiful family."

"Oh, I'm not—" Emma stopped her clarification when the girl hurried away, clearly not listening. She shrugged at Justin. "I'll set the record straight when she comes back."

"She must be new. Don't worry about it. Someone will tell her." He settled Kyle in the chair and strapped him in before hooking on the tray, then sat in the booth across the table from her. "People in Blackwater Lake talk. You've been warned."

Emma slipped off her lightweight jacket. "Understood."

She looked around at the decor. There were framed bear photos on the light yellow walls and the menus reflected the same theme with items called the Mama, Papa and Baby Bear combos. In the front half of the diner there was a counter with red-plastic-covered swivel stools. Michelle and Alan Crawford stood behind it, talking to an older man and woman seated there. Justin watched Emma studying them.

When Kyle slapped his hands on the high-chair tray, she reached into the diaper bag and pulled out a Ziploc baggie with crackers. She smiled at him and brushed the downy hair off his forehead. "Here you go, sweetie."

Justin realized that she was off the clock, so to speak,

but she didn't turn the nurturing off. It was just natural to her and something he found as sexy as it was appealing.

He glanced over his shoulder to where the diner owners stood. "They're a nice-looking couple."

"Who?" Emma looked away from Kyle and met his gaze.

"Your parents."

"This is completely surreal. Shouldn't I feel some connection to them?" There was conflict in her eyes, changing them from warm brown to almost black. "They seem like very nice people, but that's nothing more than an observation. I don't feel anything more than I would for strangers and it seems like I should since their blood is flowing through my veins."

"Sharing DNA doesn't automatically create a bond. It's the whole nature versus nurture thing. Only time can develop a relationship." Or show a guy that there isn't one, he thought, remembering how his own feelings for Kristina Bradley-Flint sputtered and died until he felt nothing but critical of the woman he'd married. "Kyle and I usually stop to chat with them when we come in. They're very friendly."

"That's how Michelle knew Kyle. When I ran into her at the grocery store," Emma reminded him.

He nodded. "They have three sons. None of them live here in Blackwater Lake."

"I have brothers?" There was shock and surprise in her voice.

"Yes. All very successful in their respective careers, according to the proud parents."

"I never thought about having siblings."

"By all accounts, Michelle and Alan did a great job raising their kids. That means after losing their youngest child and going through a parent's worst nightmare, they had the strength of character to pull it together for the sake of the children. Who all turned out to be good, productive men," he finished gently.

"What's your point?" There was an edge to her voice and she blinked. "Wow. That was abrasive. But in my own defense, this is my night off. No offense."

"None taken." He wanted to reach across the table and squeeze her hand, but, as he'd told her, everyone talked. "My point is that you come from good people."

"Like you said—that's DNA. But they didn't raise me."

Justin grabbed the menus tucked behind the salt-and-pepper holder next to the half wall separating them from the booth on the other side. He handed one to her. "What's *your* point?"

"I'm not sure. But it never crossed my mind that I might have siblings and I don't know why."

"Because you didn't know any different. You were raised an only child."

"And that's her fault."

"Who?"

"My mom—Ruth—the woman who stole me from them." She pressed her lips together, frustrated with distinguishing who was who in this bizarre scenario. Her expression changed from moment to moment, reflecting her contradictory emotions. "I loved her. She was my mother. She was also the worst kind of liar. I was raised by a woman who did the most despicable thing and lived a lie, forced me to live a lie all my life." Her eyes were bleak and anger wrapped around the words. "What does that make me?"

"An innocent victim."

"Children learn what they live. Maybe that made it easier for me not to tell the whole truth."

"The deception isn't yours to be responsible for." Justin didn't have the right words to reassure her, but every part of him rejected what she'd just said. "But I can tell you one thing."

"What?" She turned troubled eyes to his.

"Whatever else she did wrong, the way she raised you wasn't part of it. You're an honest woman."

"How do you know?"

"I could tell that keeping this to yourself took a personal toll. I can also say that you're a good and loving woman."

"How can you be sure of that?"

"The way you are with Kyle."

She glanced at the counter where the diner owners stood, then absently opened the menu on the dark-wood table between them. "She stole from me, too. It would have been nice to have big brothers."

"Why?" He handed Kyle another cracker, which the boy eagerly took.

"When someone was mean to me, they could have beat him up." She watched the little boy crumble the cracker then use both hands to sweep the pieces off the tray.

"By someone, I assume you mean the two-faced scumbag?"

"Yeah." As he'd hoped, she smiled. "I was really in a bad place after my mother confessed then died. He and I were having problems and I thought we should take a break."

"Sounds reasonable."

"It didn't last long, at least for me. I was lonely." She caught the corner of her lip between her teeth. "So I stopped by his apartment and as it turned out, *he* wasn't lonely at all."

"Another woman."

"Yeah. And I found out she wasn't the only one. He'd

been seeing other women the whole time we were engaged."

"Two-faced scumbag is too good for him." Justin hated the idea of anyone hurting her and the words came out before he could stop them. "*I* could beat him up for you."

"Really? And what about those surgeon's hands?" Her eyes brightened for a moment, then the expression faded. "Another big brother?"

"Sort of."

Justin could handle feeling like a big brother a whole lot better than what he was feeling now, which was more like a jealous boyfriend. That was all kinds of trouble. He supposed it was a plus that Emma had sworn off men. As much as he wanted to kiss her, acting on it would be the fastest way to chase her off.

So, he had to rein in his hormones, but that was easier said than done.

Chapter Five

"Seriously, Emma, if there's something else you need to do on your afternoon off, I can handle buying winter clothes for Kyle."

"It's your afternoon off, too." She looked at him with the baby in his arms and couldn't help smiling.

Three days after dinner at the diner, Emma, Kyle and Justin were ready to walk out the door and drive to the nearest mall, which wasn't all that close. Time was flying and September was ending and would soon give way to October. As Michelle had told her, the weather quickly turned cold in Montana. Several days before, there had been a light dusting of snow and Justin asked if she would help him buy winter clothes for the baby, since their respective afternoons off were the same.

This was the first time he'd asked her for a favor, and the only reason she'd even considered turning him down was because of how appealing it was to spend time with him.

"Call me crazy," she said, "but when you mentioned shopping, I could swear you looked like a man who'd rather take a sharp stick in the eye than step foot in a mall."

"I didn't think it showed."

"Oh, please." She couldn't help laughing. "Show me a guy who actually wants to shop and there's a better than even chance that he's gay."

"So given my aversion to shopping, I passed the test."

In so many ways, she thought, her heart beating just a little too fast. Fortunately, she didn't say that out loud.

"Well, I like to shop. Especially for Kyle's clothes," she said, brushing her palm over the boy's chubby cheek. "And the best part is it's *your* money."

"There's no one I'd rather spend it on." He looked at his son and there was a mother lode of tenderness softening the masculine angles of his handsome face. "What do you say, Kyle? Should we go bye-bye?"

The little boy pointed a chubby finger at the front door and jabbered, "Ba."

"I think we have a yes vote," Emma said.

"Okay, then, let's get this over with." He grinned. "What I meant to say was, let's get this show on the road."

The three of them left the house through the downstairs laundry room, which had a connecting door to the garage. Justin hit the automatic opener and the door went up, letting in the sunshine. He settled his son in the car seat of his SUV and she set the diaper bag on the rear passenger floor before getting in the front. Justin slid in behind the wheel, started the car and backed out of the driveway.

Truthfully, Emma would rather spend her afternoon off with Justin and Kyle than have time to herself. She had acquaintances in Blackwater Lake, but friendship took a while and putting in time and effort could be pointless. Her future was uncertain; she didn't know how long she would stay.

Six weeks had passed since Justin hired her and so far her crush on him showed no sign of letting up. But he'd made it clear that his feelings were more in the big-brother camp. She still didn't know whether or not to tell the Crawfords she was their daughter and had been so busy with her job, she hadn't had time to make a decision on the issue. Probably she was procrastinating, but for now she put it on the back burner.

Justin drove around the lake and headed out of town, where he guided the SUV onto the highway. Emma glanced into the rear seat and smiled.

"He's asleep already," she said. It had been her idea to leave the house around nap time to make sure the baby was rested for shopping. "How far is it to the mall?"

"About forty-five minutes."

"Good."

"Really?" He glanced at her, one eyebrow raised. "Most women would be euphoric if shopping was in their backyard."

"I'm not most women."

"Tell me something I don't know."

His voice sounded a little raspy and wrapped in male appreciation, although a quick glance didn't confirm. There was a muscle jumping in his jaw, but dark aviator sunglasses hid the expression in his eyes. Did he just pay her a compliment? Her own feelings being so close to the tipping point, she decided it was best not to go there.

"Don't get me wrong," she said. "I have nothing against shopping. And this is my afternoon off, but I still have my nanny hat on."

"It looks good on you." He glanced over for a moment, but his expression was still impossible to read.

Again she heard huskiness in his tone, but chalked it up to altitude and cold air. That was safer.

"My point is, and I do have one," she persisted, "Kyle

will get in his nap. As we discussed. That means this expedition will go smoothly. Our little angel—"

The words sank in and she stopped, appalled that she'd said that to the man who'd made it clear the first time they met that he didn't want to be a we, us or our. "I meant to say *your* little angel. That wasn't flirting, I swear. It's just that I'm attached to him. In a professional way. Really, Justin, that was an unprofessional thing for me to say and you shouldn't be concerned that—"

"Take a breath." He slid her a brief look and the corners of his mouth curved up. "Don't worry about it. I'm glad you care about him."

"I do, but—"

"No buts. I have an idea. You're off and I'm off. For the rest of the day we'll just be friends shopping together."

The tension in Justin's voice had disappeared, leaving behind a teasing and carefree mood. So, for today, she was making a conscious and deliberate choice to relax and have fun.

The problem was, it would be easy to cross the invisible line into personal territory and that was a no-no. There was a risk to letting go of traditional boss-employee roles and sliding into something more casual. But to say that out loud would lead to a place too delicate to navigate without revealing her simmering feelings.

"Okay," she said. "Friends for the afternoon."

Forty-five minutes later, when Justin drove into the mall parking lot, she couldn't believe they were already here. She'd had so much friendly fun talking with him, the time had flown.

As she'd done every few minutes, she glanced in the backseat. "He's still asleep. Maybe I can get him out without waking him and he can have a little more rest."

"Okay." He drove the outer perimeter mall road until

seeing the store he wanted, then turned left into an aisle and guided the car between the white lines of a parking space. "Here we are."

"Here" was a big warehouse of a store that specialized in all-weather outdoor gear for the whole family. She'd been told by mom acquaintances in Kyle's weekly play group that it had the best selection of warm clothes for a child his age.

Emma got out of the car as quietly as possible and waited while Justin removed the stroller from the back and unfolded it. When all was ready, he nodded, giving her the go-ahead. "Here goes nothing." She opened the rear passenger door and gently released the car seat's restraint closure before lifting the baby out and setting him in the stroller. He squirmed some but didn't wake up and she quickly belted him in and snuggled a blanket around him.

Standing on tiptoe, she whispered in Justin's ear, "I can't believe he's still asleep."

"You've got the magic touch."

The husky tone sent shivers dancing over her skin that had nothing to do with winter and everything to do with heat. It was one of those forbidden feelings that came without warning and were happening more frequently.

"There's no telling how long we've got, so let's roll," she said quickly.

"You're the expert."

While Justin pushed the stroller, she quickly moved across the pedestrian crosswalk and into the store, trying to forget how good he smelled and how easy it would have been to lean into him. Inside, there was a lot to distract her. The warehouse had racks of jackets and snow pants, recessed cubbyholes stacked with sweaters and thermal shirts and long underwear.

Knit hats and gloves were everywhere. Overhead signs

directed them to the infant and toddler section, where Kyle's size was located. The sheer volume of choice was overwhelming. They were standing between racks of tiny jackets and heavier clothing appropriate for really brutal cold weather.

Bewildered, Justin looked at her. "Boy, am I glad you've got a master's degree in this stuff."

"Just to keep things real, I never took a class dedicated to the finer points of dressing a baby for winter in Montana. The way I see it, this is all about common sense." She headed for the jackets.

"Wait." Justin stood with his hands on the stroller but didn't push it. "We should look at snowsuits."

"I don't think he'll need that."

"Really?" He slid his sunglasses to the top of his head. "People in Blackwater Lake tell me the temperature can drop to below freezing."

"But Kyle is too little to be out in weather like that."

"What if you have to take him to the doctor or grocery store?"

Emma thought it over. "We go from house to car to building. All heated or protected from the worst cold."

"But what if we build a snowman or have a snowball fight?" Justin persisted.

He was taking paternal protection to a new and endearing place where practicality didn't go. She couldn't help smiling at him. "He's not even walking just yet."

"Almost."

"Be that as it may, I highly doubt that he'll be outside long enough to warrant a snowsuit."

"I don't know." He rubbed the back of his neck and scanned the abundance of warm outerwear. "It seems like he should have it just in case."

"Certainly you can get whatever you want," she said, "but if that's the case, why did you ask me to come along?"

"For an educated opinion. So what do you think? And remember, money is no object."

Her eyes narrowed as she read between the lines of what he'd just said. "You want me to tell you it's okay to buy both."

"Not true." Although the amusement in his eyes hinted that he was busted. "I don't need your permission."

"Of course not. But that doesn't change what you want to hear. You can buy out the whole toddler department, but it won't prove anything about your parenting skills."

"That's not what I'm doing."

"Yes, it is. For the record, let me say—in my expert opinion—you're a fantastic father, Justin. But what you're suggesting is impractical. If you get something that will fit for a couple of years, it will be too big and bulky for him to move easily. If it fits now, he'll outgrow it for next year. That just seems wasteful."

"So what? Call it doing my part for a sluggish economy. I—"

"Excuse me, but I couldn't help overhearing."

Emma turned at the sound of the voice behind her. A saleswoman in her mid- to late-twenties had joined them. Her long brown hair was shot through with red highlights and she smiled pleasantly. Her manner was very professional, although she did let slip one appreciative female glance in Justin's direction. Emma couldn't fault her; he was an exceptionally good-looking man.

Her name tag said Peg. "I couldn't help noticing that you're having a parental difference of opinion."

"Oh, we're not—" Emma rethought what she'd been about to say. "Well, he's the father—"

"Yes, he is. The resemblance is unmistakable."

Justin jumped in. "The thing is, Peg, I know you're in sales and would happily sell us the whole department, but what do you think is best for cold-weather protection for a one-year-old?"

"The baby is too little to spend an extended length of time outside in weather too cold for any sensible human being," Emma interrupted. "Don't you think?"

Peg indulgently smiled at each of them. "This isn't the first time I've had to referee parents."

To his credit, Justin didn't correct her and pull rank. "What do most of them do?"

"After a difference of opinion, when they end up buying more than is really necessary for their child, I'm pretty sure they go home to kiss and make up." She laughed, then studied the sleeping baby. "He's an incredibly beautiful child. Such a combination of you two."

"Thanks." Justin looked amused by the comment and still didn't correct her. "So, we're originally from California. What do you think?"

"He'll need a snowsuit."

"Okay," he said. "Then that's what we'll look at."

"I'll leave you to it," Peg said. "Let me know if you have any more questions."

When the woman was far enough away that she couldn't hear and assume another parental argument, Emma said, "Go ahead. You can say I told you so."

Justin grinned. "Would I do that?"

"You should." She shook her head. "And you should have told her we're not married."

"She would have thought my son was born out of wedlock."

"So? No one thinks anything about that these days. Or you could have told her the truth. That I'm the nanny."

"Not this afternoon," he reminded her.

"Right." For a few hours they were friends. She looked at the little boy just starting to wake up. He opened his eyes, lifting the thick, dark lashes fanning his pink cheeks. "I'm incredibly flattered that anyone would think a child as beautiful as Kyle was mine. I can't believe it."

"I can." There was a fierce, hungry expression in his eyes before he looked away. "What I mean is that you're so natural with him, no one would guess you're not his mom."

That was a good save and she was grateful. "Thank you for saying that."

The truth was that caring for Kyle came naturally to her because she was genuinely fond of him. She didn't have to work at it.

"That's not flattery," Justin said. "Just a fact. And I'll do whatever I can to make him happy. And he's happy with you as his nanny."

This time there was no huskiness in his voice; any need, real or imagined, had disappeared from his eyes. He was all business. She should have been appreciative of another reminder that she needed to keep her feelings in check or risk them being crushed.

Later, when she went from friend back to nanny, she'd find a way to work up the appropriate level of gratitude. For a little while she'd felt as if she was part of a family, and going back to being the hired help wouldn't be easy after getting a small taste of everything she'd ever wanted.

While Justin and Kyle answered the door, Emma sat on the edge of the sofa in the family room feeling like a bump on a pickle. It was the baby's first birthday. Friends had been invited to the celebration because Justin was an only child and his parents were deceased. There was no extended family.

She wasn't family *or* friend, just the nanny, but he'd

overruled any misgivings and asked her to join them. She wanted to be a part of celebrating this momentous first birthday but felt like an intruder, filling an empty place that wasn't hers to fill. It felt like overstepping, something for which she would be judged in a bad way.

But Justin was the boss. Voices drifted to her and she stood just before the boss walked into the room with his friends.

"I'll do the introductions." Justin put Kyle on the rug and he crawled over to her to be picked up. "Emma Robbins, this is Camille Halliday and her fiancé, Ben McKnight."

She lifted the little boy into her arms, then moved closer and shook hands with both of them. "It's nice to meet you."

"Likewise." Camille studied her. "You're so pretty. Ben, don't you think she looks like that actress? The one who blindsided her superstar husband with a divorce then moved with their daughter to New York?"

Her fiancé hesitated, obviously trying to pick his words carefully. "I don't keep up with celebrity stuff. If it's not a revolutionary new procedure to repair a shattered ankle…" He shrugged.

"Don't pay any attention to my friend the hotel heiress," Justin told her. "You can take the girl out of L.A., but you can't take L.A. out of the girl. That's where Cam and I met."

"Not because I had work done." The other woman looked down at her chest, perfectly displayed in an expensive black knit dress. It also showcased her small baby bump. "This bosom has only recently become impressive and I give credit where credit is due."

"And where would that be?" Emma asked.

"The baby."

"What about me?" Ben's voice was teasing. "I had a role in the process."

"Since this is your baby, you do get some credit. That way you can't complain when it eventually disappears."

"Never happen." The love shining in his eyes left no doubt he was telling the truth. He was holding a gift wrapped in blue paper with red fire trucks covering it. "And this is for the birthday boy."

Emma envied the two, who were clearly in love and starting a family. She smiled at the little boy in her arms, just a bit sad that other people's children might very well be the only ones in her life.

"That's for you, Kyle." She smiled when he stared at the present, then wiggled to be put down.

"What can I get everyone to drink?" Justin asked.

"Beer for me." Ben glanced at his wife.

"Nothing alcoholic or caffeinated. For obvious reasons." Cam absently rubbed her belly. "I miss coffee more than I can say."

"Club soda with lime. Wine for you, Em?"

She knew that was Justin's subtle way of saying he had no problem with it. "That would be nice."

"Okay. I'll be right back. Talk among yourselves."

Since the large family room was adjacent to the kitchen, he could hear every word. But for several moments there weren't any. The three of them watched Kyle trying to figure out how to unwrap his package. When he slapped it several times, Emma knew his patience was fading fast and there would be a loud protest any second.

"Do you mind if I help him a little?" She looked at the couple who were watching, estimating their reaction to the suggestion. "He's getting frustrated. I'll just tear one end a bit to give him the idea."

"Please." Cam smiled tenderly when Emma slid a finger under one of the corners and pulled loose enough paper for the baby to grab and rip to his heart's content. "Ben told me it would take SEAL Team Six to extract that box from all the tape I put on."

"Don't be too disappointed if he has more fun with the paper than with what's inside." She observed as the child happily ripped paper away, leaving the wide ribbon and three-dimensional red bow still attached. "At this age it's the simple things that entertain them. Sticks, rocks, empty boxes."

Eventually a box emerged with the picture of a block set, complete with figures of doctor and nurse. It was age appropriate for safety, but clearly Kyle was more interested in happily tearing wrapping paper to shreds.

Ben sighed. "I think we have a lot to learn."

"You'll do fine." Justin walked over with a tray holding their drinks. "Cam and I actually met at a fund-raiser for a children's hospital in Los Angeles."

"That's right." Camille took the glass of club soda he handed her. "It was one of those galas where the rich and famous give away gobs of money in exchange for positive public opinion and tax write-offs."

"Sometimes they have a passion for the cause," Justin reminded her.

"Mostly not." Cam gave him a pointed look. "And I know this because I went to a lot of them for atonement. It took time and money to make people forget or at least forgive my teenage transgressions."

Emma finally realized who she was. "You're *that* hotel heiress."

The other woman sighed. "Guilty."

"The only thing you're guilty of is being a teenager. We've all been young and stupid." Justin set the tray on the coffee table and grabbed his beer. "Why don't you sit?"

"Are you saying I'm old?"

"I'm saying you're pregnant."

The couple took seats side by side on the full-size sofa and Justin sat on the shorter one at a right angle to them. The only place for Emma was beside him and when she put herself there, their thighs brushed. His gaze jumped to hers for a charged moment then they both quickly looked away. Camille's shrewd expression said she hadn't missed the exchange and the jury was still out on whether or not she approved.

Justin cleared his throat. "I actually have Cam to thank for the fact that I'm here in Blackwater Lake."

Emma felt like gulping the white wine he'd given her but forced herself to sip. "Oh?"

He nodded. "She's been in town since January."

"I drew the short family straw and was given the assignment of turning a profit at Blackwater Lake Lodge. At first I thought I'd been exiled to a foreign country and the employees treated me like an alien." She smiled at her fiancé. "Everything changed when I met Ben."

"His specialty is orthopedics, so she had inside information on the medical position that opened up at the clinic and passed the information on to me," Justin explained. "I just had to wait until the building project to expand Mercy Medical Clinic was complete, then I got the job. Now Ben and I work together."

"Speaking of expansion," the other man said. "Cam and I aren't the only ones working on a family. My brother, Alex, and his fiancée, Ellie, are expecting a baby just a couple months after us."

"A toast to the McKnights." Justin held up his long-neck bottle and they all touched their glasses.

Cam leaned back and rested a hand on her baby bump. "What brought you to Blackwater Lake, Emma?"

She should have expected the question but hadn't. She wasn't prepared. "Wow. Where to start."

Justin had not only kept her secret, he'd supported her during this confusing time. But if she told anyone else, the news could get out in a way she couldn't control.

She glanced at Kyle, for once wishing he would have an immediate need for a dirty-diaper change. But he was happily enthralled with unraveling his ribbon.

"Emma came here on vacation." Justin's expression said he had her back. "Hawaii's loss is Montana's gain."

She was disturbed and relieved in equal parts. He'd covered for her but she'd never considered that confiding in him would compromise his honesty. Still, she couldn't help liking him a whole lot more for the gallant gesture.

"That's true," she agreed. "I'd wanted to visit Montana and settled on Blackwater Lake."

"She liked it so much, she decided to stay." Justin took a drink from his beer. "It was my good fortune she did. Sylvia was leaving with or without a replacement and Emma is great with Kyle. Not to mention a seriously good cook."

"Really?" Cam shifted on the sofa, trying to get comfortable.

"Absolutely. And it's the little things she does," he continued.

"The way to a man's heart is through his stomach." Ben grinned when his friend choked as he was taking a drink.

"If that were true," Cam said, giving her fiancé a look, "you wouldn't be the father of this baby. I run a hotel and cooking isn't part of my skills set." She met Justin's gaze. "So tell me about the little things she does."

Justin thought for a moment. "Take Kyle's birthday. The menu tonight is all about his favorites. Macaroni and cheese. Green beans."

"I made a chicken dish, too, for the adults," Emma said.

"Sounds yummy."

"It is." Justin rested his forearms on his knees. "She

made the birthday cake from scratch, too. And baked a little one just for him."

Emma picked it up from there. "He can eat it, play with it, wear it or throw it on the floor. This is his day to be the man, in his one-year-old way."

"Who's cleaning up?" Ben wanted to know.

"Me," she said. "The parameters are broad, but I draw the line at smearing cake on the windows."

"Aw." Cam's expression went all gooey. "I'd never have thought of that."

"A kid is only one once."

"That does it." Cam looked at Ben. "When Delaney is born, I'm stealing Emma for our nanny."

"Is that a girl name?" Justin grinned.

"Yes," the parents-to-be said together.

Then Cam smiled and added, "When our children grow up, maybe they'll fall in love and Kyle will propose. I'd love that because we could pick our little girl's in-laws."

"You're such a romantic," Justin teased. "Were you always that way or is it pregnancy hormones?"

"Some of both. And don't think you distracted me." She looked at Emma. "Will you consider a job offer?"

"Never say never. But it would have to be pretty spectacular." She smiled as Kyle held her leg and pulled himself to a standing position. "This little guy has stolen my heart."

She loved him; it was as simple as that. Her feelings for Justin were far more complicated. There was always the acute attraction, but more than that was his loyalty and sense of honor. She was incredibly grateful to him for compromising his truthfulness in order to protect her secret. That suddenly made it more urgent to figure out her personal situation.

She owed it to Justin to settle her life so that he could settle his.

Chapter Six

Justin couldn't believe that Halloween was only two weeks away. "I'm really glad you talked me into coming to the pumpkin patch."

"I didn't talk you into anything," Emma retorted. "It was merely a suggestion and you seized the moment to start Flint-family traditions. And rightly so."

It was a clear but chilly night as Justin pushed Kyle's stroller on the dirt path past the bales of hay and displays of ghosts, witches and zombies. It was all set up in a field just a couple streets over from Main, where, in about six weeks, there would be Christmas trees.

"Well, someone was talked into something." He snapped his fingers. "Oh, right, that was me talking you into coming along with us."

He wasn't sure why it was any more important than helping him shop for a jacket or being part of his son's first birthday celebration, but it was. So he made sure she was here.

"Make fun if you feel better." Her chin lifted a notch and just made her look cuter with her cream-colored, pom-

pom-topped knit hat. Her hands were shoved into the pockets of a puffy pink jacket as they walked past a fun house and its weird chain-rattling sounds, thumps and screams.

"I'm not making fun. Just giving credit where credit is due." He glanced at her, and his fingers tingled with the urge to run them through all that shiny brown hair tumbling down from underneath her hat.

"It really wasn't a creditworthy situation," she protested. "Halloween is coming and I saw a flyer at the grocery store. Every kid should have a pumpkin and make a project of carving it. Never too early to start traditions."

"I couldn't agree more. The thing is, I get busy with work, and stuff like this could slide under my radar if not for you."

The path was crowded with people; there was excitement in the air. Children were chasing each other and some had their faces painted with pumpkins, bats or scarecrows. Adults followed their kids, called out to slow them down if they got too far ahead.

Justin wanted Kyle to be a part of this but wasn't good at being aware when it was going on. He wasn't sexist, but events like face painting and haunted houses fell into the female sphere of expertise. Since he got so easily wrapped up in a demanding job, Emma was necessary for balance in his son's life.

He was a single father raising a child alone.

He glanced at her and the overhead spotlights showed her frown. It was an ongoing struggle to keep her from seeing that he wanted her more every day. Maybe that leaked out in what he'd just said. If not for her...

"What's wrong?" he asked.

"Nothing."

"Then why are you making that face?"

She met his gaze, her expression wiped clean of any emotion. "What face?"

"The one you were making before going deliberately blank."

He studied the smooth skin on her forehead where the frown had been and the realization came out of the blue as it so often did. She was so beautiful that sometimes it was like a punch to the gut. And he couldn't let her know.

"Look, Emma, I know faces. It's my job. So come clean. What's bothering you? If I did something…"

"No. Gosh, no, Justin." Their shoulders brushed and for a moment she put her hand on his arm. "It's not about you. I was just remembering my mother bringing me to pick out a pumpkin. Every year, I think, until I went to college."

He figured she meant the woman who'd kidnapped her. "Not a good memory?"

"Just the opposite. It was wonderful." The frown was back. "But because I had them with her, Michelle and Alan didn't have them with their daughter."

Justin wondered if she realized she was talking about herself in the third person. She was still conflicted about her loyalty to the woman she loved, the same one who'd done a horrible thing and hurt a lot of people, including Emma. And because Emma made Kyle's life practically perfect, Justin sometimes forgot that she had an agenda that wasn't necessarily compatible with his.

He stopped the stroller and put a hand on her arm. Troubled brown eyes held his own. "I'm going to tell you three things that you probably already know. But it never hurts to hear them out loud."

"Okay." It looked as if she was bracing herself.

"Number one—what happened isn't your fault. Next—it officially sucks what happened to you. Finally, and most important, you don't need to figure things out tonight."

The corners of her mouth curved up just a fraction, but as the words sank in she smiled and it was beautiful to see. Like a sunny day after a storm.

"You're right." She nodded emphatically. "Now who should get credit where credit is due?"

"Shucks, ma'am—"

She laughed and shook her head at the silliness. "If Beverly Hills could only see you now."

Before she could finish the thought, Kyle let out a wail at the same time he was doing his best Houdini imitation, trying to get free of the stroller belt holding him in. When his efforts didn't work, the verbal complaints escalated to a pitch that would make a dog cringe.

"Better get moving," he said.

"I'm with you."

Justin pushed forward, but the little boy didn't let up and the protest got louder, which hadn't seemed possible. He started leaning to the side, trying to get out.

"He's so over the stroller," Emma said. "I think he needs a break."

They stopped beside several huge crates filled with pumpkins for sale. "This seems like a good place."

"I agree." Emma unbelted the little boy and lifted him out, but he didn't want to be held, either. He whined and tried to wiggle out of her hold.

Justin wouldn't complain if she was holding him. Her arms were a place he'd imagined being too many times to count, but he had a completely different perspective on the issue.

Emma looked at him, the corner of her full bottom lip caught between her teeth. "Okay, don't do a father freak-out about where I'm about to put him. There's grass here. I'm just going to set him on the ground, give him a little space."

"I'm trying to decide whether or not I resent the freak-out remark," he teased. "Which one of us used antiseptic wipes on a perfectly clean high chair at the Grizzly Bear Diner? Just saying…"

"The diner is a public restaurant. Different children sit in those chairs with runny noses and heaven knows what other germs. You don't know that it was perfectly clean," she said as if that explained everything.

Without another word, she set Kyle on the grass and he looked happy as could be. Immediately he crawled over to the cardboard crate and put a hand on it, for leverage to stand up.

"Okay," Justin said, "we might as well pick out a pumpkin now. How do you know if it's a good one?"

"Didn't you ever do this with your parents?"

"Yeah. But it was a long time ago."

She sighed as if he were dull as dirt. "It's all about shape. And remember, a face is getting carved out of this." She grabbed a plump, round one. "Faces are your business, Doctor. What would you do with this one?"

He studied it for a few moments, then touched the widest part of the curve. "First I'd use my scalpel here and here for defined cheekbones."

Emma nodded her approval. "I can see that. If we use a carrot for a nose?"

"I think that's more a snowman thing, but let's go with it." He walked from one side to the other, pretending to assess. "I'd take a potato peeler to that pointy thing and try to soften the tip."

"Harsh." Emma laughed, then picked up another one that was narrower, elongated. "And what about this one?"

He glanced at Kyle, who was bouncing even though barely touching the box for balance. His little boy was essentially standing on his own. Good man.

Then he looked back at the pumpkin. "This guy needs a chin. The forehead is a little high, but we can distract from that by drawing focus here." He indicated the bottom. "Every guy wants a granite jaw."

"Every guy?" She looked at him as if assessing his chin. "I don't think I'd change a thing if I were you."

In his head Justin knew she was teasing, but the rest of his body went tight and hard at the compliment. Obviously he cared too much what she thought when she looked at him. And she must have seen something on his face, because her smile slipped and she quickly looked away.

"What do you think about this one, Kyle?" she asked, plucking a pumpkin from the pile and putting it on the ground.

The little boy gurgled as he removed his small hand from the crate and took one step, then another without holding on to anything. He stood on his own, a little unsteadily, beside the big, orange pumpkin.

"Did you see what I saw?" Her voice was calm, but Emma's eyes were bright with excitement that had nothing to do with her job.

Justin knew that because it felt as if that same thrill was on his own face. "I think he just took his first steps. What do you think?"

She stood when the little boy braced himself on the pumpkin. "Definitely his first steps." And then she threw herself into his arms. "Oh, my gosh, Justin. He's walking."

"I know."

And he was excited about that, too. But damn it, Emma felt so good in his arms, pink jacket, funky hat and all. He couldn't help himself and pulled her in tighter for full body contact. Being this close to her had him thinking about long, slow kisses in his bed. There was no question that he started breathing faster and it wasn't his imagination that Emma was, too. He saw it when she stepped away and couldn't look at him.

"It's getting cold," she said.

Justin hadn't noticed. He was hot all over and wanted to do something about it.

"We need to get Kyle home."

"Yeah." His house wasn't the neutral territory it had once been, Justin realized. Emma had made it a home.

Damn this gray area where he was living. He wanted her more than he'd ever wanted a woman in his life. But she was his employee and clearly very fond of his son. Just a while ago he'd reminded himself that she had other concerns in her life beyond her job.

She was really good at being a nanny and he'd been lucky to find her in this small town. He hated the thought of her leaving, hated that Kyle would be affected by the change. But she *was* an employee.

She could be replaced.

The morning after the pumpkin patch Emma was tired because she hadn't slept well. Almost kissing your boss who didn't want to be kissed tended to keep a nanny up most of the night. Although, if she was honest, he *had* pulled her closer when she hugged him. His breathing had quickened, too, and what did she do with that information?

Nothing if she wanted to keep her job.

And today her job was about Kyle's play group at Blackwater Lake Early Childhood Learning Center. It was located on Main, just down the street from the Grizzly Bear Diner, nestled between Tanya's Treasures and Potter's Ice-Cream Parlor. The class was technically Mommy and Me, but Emma figured the fact she wasn't his biological mother didn't matter.

She pulled the car into the rear lot utilized by customers of all businesses that faced Main Street. Her gaze automatically went to the diner where *her* biological parents worked and managed their business. It weighed heavily on her that she still hadn't made up her mind what to do, and being sleep deprived didn't help. As Justin said, she didn't have to decide today and gave herself permission to table the issue until she wasn't so tired.

Maybe there would be a sign from the universe when the time was right. Or she had to face the fact that a fear she didn't understand was standing in her way.

"Here we are, big guy." Emma turned off the ignition, then exited the car. She smiled at the memory of this little heartbreaker-in-training always gravitating to little Danielle Potter, a beautiful child who was also a year old. "Maybe your little friend will be here today."

"Ga—"

She opened the passenger door and grinned at him. "I'll take that as a 'Wow, I hope so.'"

After getting him out of the car seat, she reached for the diaper bag and slid the strap over her shoulder. "And you get to show off today, mister. You're the man. Taking your first steps is a very big deal."

A first kiss from Justin would have been a big deal, too, but not in a good way.

"You're getting heavier every day, pal." She moved through the parking lot toward the center's backdoor. "It's a good thing you're starting to walk. Your daddy doesn't have a problem lifting you because he's strong."

Emma shivered at the thought, but chalked it up to the cloudy gray sky and chilly wind that blew from the north.

"Da—"

"Yes, Da." She kissed his cheek. "You are too cute. Go easy on Danielle. I like her and her mom."

After opening the door, Emma moved past the office

and storeroom to the big open play area where a quick glance told her the majority of moms and babies were already gathered. She stopped at the cubbies on the wall and removed Kyle's jacket then stored it along with the diaper bag.

A few moments later, she took the last empty spot in the play circle and sat cross-legged on the floor with Kyle in her lap. Maggie and Danielle were to her left.

There was no teacher for this particular class; it was about moms and babies socializing and the children learning to share. The toys were blocks, simple four-to-six-piece wooden puzzles and shapes to introduce basics and increase major muscle development. She'd been to a few sessions and was getting to know the mothers, who seemed to be accepting her.

"Hi, everyone," she said, glancing around. There was a chorus of greetings in response. "How are you, Maggie?"

"Good. Look, Danielle—Kyle is here." She dropped a kiss on the top of her daughter's head. "What's up, Emma?"

"Not much," she lied.

"You look tired."

"Maybe a little." Wow, was this woman perceptive.

Maggie was a pretty brunette, petite and fragile-looking, but looks could be deceiving. She was a widow; her husband had been a soldier and died in Afghanistan several months before his daughter was born. It took a lot of strength to get through that alone and run a business, too. And she always seemed cheerful, although her beautiful brown eyes held a soul-deep sadness.

The sadness disappeared when a gleam stole into those eyes. "So, taking this little guy to the pumpkin patch last night wore you out?"

The only way she could know that was if she'd been there. "I didn't see you."

"I saw *you*." The teasing tone implied she'd seen more than that.

"Me, too." Lindsay Griffin watched her ten-month-old son crawl toward the toys in the center of the group. A blue-eyed redhead wearing square black glasses, she had the eager look of feminine curiosity. "What's it like to live with hunky Dr. Flint?"

Emma felt her cheeks burn as she realized at least two of these women had seen her hugging Justin. Why hadn't she noticed them?

Duh. She'd been a little preoccupied trying to ignore the fact that he'd held her just a little too long. After that, she was concerned with doing damage control. Trying not to get fired after letting her emotions get out of control had been her priority. But apparently there was still more damage control to do.

She glanced around the circle. Half the moms closest to her waited impatiently for her answer. The other half were too far away to hear and were chatting among themselves.

"I'm not living with Justin. He hired me to care for Kyle."

Maggie held her daughter's hands as the little girl in her pink flowered dress and white tights stood. "Correct me if I'm wrong, but the two of you occupy space under the same roof, no?"

"Yes."

"Then you're living with him," Lindsay said, like a trial lawyer who got something out of a hostile witness. "How is it?"

"A job," she answered carefully.

"So you are attracted," the redhead persisted.

"I didn't say that, either." She helped Kyle stand, then let his hands rest on her palms so he had the illusion of holding on.

"Do you have a boyfriend?" Plump, blonde Rachel Evans hugged her look-alike, curly-haired daughter, Casey.

"No." Emma saw no point in adding that she'd been engaged and it didn't go well.

"So there's nothing standing in your way if you decided to go with the attraction," Lindsay chimed in.

Maybe she *should* share a few details to throw them off the scent. Evidence that she had no interest in anything serious. "I was engaged in California but he was cheating on me."

"Jerk." Lindsay turned up her nose.

"Actually, that's too good for him. He's a scumbag weasel dog," Emma clarified and they laughed.

"I'm sensing that you're not in the mood for love." Maggie looked as if she understood not wanting to go there.

"Exactly." Emma nodded for emphasis. "Especially with my employer. Very unprofessional."

"Let me get this straight." Lindsay pushed her glasses up more firmly on her nose when her little guy knocked them off center. "You live in the same house and care for his son. There's cooking and light housekeeping involved."

"That's right."

"What do you get out of it?"

"A paycheck," she answered dryly.

"Of course, but—" Lindsay tucked a strand of red hair behind her ear. "Isn't it a lot like being married without the fringe benefits?"

"No. He's my boss and pays me very generously to take care of this beautiful little boy." She watched Kyle and Danielle crawl to the center of the circle and pick up blocks, then hold them out to each other.

Emma looked past Maggie and met the redhead's gaze. "Even if I were interested, he's not. He's a grieving widower and may never want another relationship."

"Good point." The sad look was back in Maggie's eyes and she nodded her understanding. Better than anyone here she knew how much love and loss hurt.

"I've heard that a man who's been married once is more likely to take the plunge again," Lindsay said.

"I don't get the impression that Justin is open to that." Emma remembered her first interview when he came right out and said he wasn't looking for a wife. However, sharing that information wasn't something she would do. "It's just a job."

"That's not what it looked like in the pumpkin patch last night." Lindsay stared over the top of her glasses.

"Kyle took his first steps. That was exciting." She was telling most of the truth.

"It looked awfully personal." Lindsay's expression indicated she expected all the details. "It seems to me—"

"All right, give Emma a break," Maggie interrupted good-naturedly. "Let's change the subject. Is Ryder still waking up every night? He could be teething."

Thank God the conversation shifted from her, and Emma sent Maggie a grateful look. The subject had changed but Emma couldn't stop thinking about it. Hugging Justin was a fringe benefit that she'd be better off without because the memory of it was driving her crazy.

She loved Kyle so much and leaving him would be very hard. But falling for his father would make the current situation even worse. It was frustrating because she'd done her best to put distance between them. Then she promptly forgot all of that and threw herself into his arms in the excitement of a baby's first steps. If he hadn't hugged her back, she'd just be embarrassed. Now she was all kinds of confused.

The rest of the playtime hour flew by and before she knew it, the session was over. The moms said goodbye and picked up their babies to leave. But Kyle and Danielle were still happily playing on the floor.

Maggie stood and smiled. "They're so sweet together, aren't they?"

"I know what you mean. They do seem to have a special bond."

"I hate to break this up, but I'm pretty sure the learning center will need the space for the toddlers in the next class."

Emma laughed. "These two would get mowed down by the bigger kids."

"That could ruin their whole day." Maggie looked at her watch. "It's almost noon. Why don't we take them to get something to eat?"

"You're not working today?"

"After lunch. I drop Danielle off at my mom's before going to the ice-cream parlor. I'll need to get something into both of us before that."

"If you're sure, I'd love to." Emma liked this woman a lot and felt they could be friends if she stayed. And if she didn't, that would be one more thing to regret. But, again, not today. "Where?"

Maggie tapped her lip. "You know the Grizzly Bear Diner is only a couple doors up, so we can walk. We don't have to load the kids into car seats to get somewhere and the food is good. Any objections?"

More than you could possibly know, Emma thought before saying, "Let's do it."

Chapter Seven

Emma walked into the Grizzly Bear Diner and automatically looked at the counter where Michelle and Alan Crawford spent a lot of time talking to the regulars. They weren't there, probably because there were no customers occupying the swivel chairs. It was just after the breakfast crowd and before the lunch rush, which meant the owners might not be here and she was sort of hoping she didn't have to see them. She wasn't ready yet.

Wendy, the thirtysomething hostess, showed them to a booth before bringing over two high chairs. With Kyle in one arm resting on her hip, she dropped the diaper bag on the booth bench seat and pulled out an antiseptic wipe. Then she proceeded to wash the plastic high chair tray and laughed when she saw Maggie doing the same thing.

Emma said to the hostess, "This isn't about not trusting you to clean off every last microbe. It's the only way to be sure."

"I'm not judging," Wendy answered, clearly not insulted. "It's a mom thing. What can I get you?"

"Coffee?" She looked at the other woman, who nodded.

"Coming right up. Your server will be with you shortly."

"Thanks."

"A mom thing," Maggie commented thoughtfully, settling Danielle in the chair. She fastened the strap and arranged the tray so it was snug but not too tight. When she looked up there was a gleam in her eyes. "She's new in town. Otherwise she would know you're the hunky doctor's nanny."

"Actually, not *his* nanny. I take care of Kyle."

"Whatever." Maggie waved her hand in dismissal. "You're an awesome nanny or she wouldn't have mistaken you for Kyle's mom. You take good care of him."

"It's what I'm paid to do."

"Technically. But there's an obvious emotional connection, too."

"I have a connection with all the children I'm responsible for."

"Okay. I won't push the issue," Maggie said. "But it's there for all the world to see."

Emma settled the little boy in his chair and gave him a cracker to keep him busy. He immediately handed it to the baby girl in the chair right next to his. The two of them were side by side at the end of the booth.

"Is that the sweetest thing?" Maggie's expression turned tender. "He's going to leave a trail of broken hearts behind him when he grows up and I just hope he spares my daughter."

"They'll be good buddies." Emma didn't think she would be around to see it, though. "That's so much better than anything romantic."

"No kidding." The other woman's dark eyes filled with a wistful sorrow when she looked at Danielle. "Never falling in love means a lot less crying."

"Yeah. That's sort of my motto." Emma's heart twisted

as she looked at the young woman across the table from her and realized she'd been through so much worse. "I'm so sorry about your husband."

"You know about Danny." It wasn't a question.

"I brought Kyle into the shop for frozen yogurt and talked to Diane and Norm Schurr. They told me about him."

"My regulars. Older couple who keep fit and come in for a treat once a week," Maggie said. "I think they just want to check up on me."

"Nice couple." They had the love, respect and years together that most people yearned for. "We started chatting and, just so you know, I did tell them I'm not Kyle's mother."

"Honesty is the best policy."

Mostly, Emma thought. She glanced past Maggie to the diner counter, but still didn't see either Michelle or Alan. Her stomach knotted and she did her best to hide it.

"Diane pointed out the picture hanging on the wall behind the cash register of you and your husband, taken the day Potter's Ice-Cream Parlor opened."

Maggie smiled, a faraway expression in her eyes. "He loved ice cream and there wasn't anything like it in Blackwater Lake. So, when we were looking to start a business, that's what we did. He was here at the grand opening and had about six months left until getting out of the army." She handed Danielle a cracker and the corners of her mouth turned up when the little girl gave it to Kyle. "Danny was so excited about becoming a father."

As words of comfort went through Emma's mind, she immediately dismissed each one. She met the other woman's gaze.

"I'm sure you've heard all the platitudes. He's her guardian angel. Watching over both of you from heaven. He's in a better place." She shook her head in frustration, remembering how it was after her mother died. "People mean well and are just trying to console. But, Maggie, it officially sucks that you were robbed of a life with him and your daughter is going to grow up without knowing her father."

"Thank you for that." Maggie looked genuinely amused. "I'm so tired of people feeling sorry for me. I hate that the whole town thinks of me as 'the widow.'"

"So, you're ready to move on?"

"It's not something you get ready for. I had a baby. Under the circumstances you just do it."

Emma looked at the two little ones happily chattering in a language only a one-year-old could understand. The father of this little boy was a widower. "You and Justin both understand how it feels to lose a spouse. Maybe—"

Maggie held up a hand. "Don't go there. I'm doing great without yucky love stuff messing everything up."

"Don't hold back. Tell me how you really feel."

The other woman laughed. "And I'll tell you something else. I like you, Emma Robbins."

"The feeling is mutual."

But Emma experienced a surge of relief that her friend wasn't interested in Justin. Jealousy wasn't a very good foundation for friendship. And friendship wasn't something she'd anticipated when making the decision to stay in town a little longer. Not that she was isolating herself on the English moors like a gothic heroine from a Charlotte Brontë novel. But the longer she was here, the more regrets she would have about leaving people behind when she was gone.

"Good." Maggie leaned forward, a conspiratorial gesture. "Because I'd like to talk to you. There's something I've been thinking about."

"Oh?"

"The crafts store next to Potter's parlor just closed its doors forever. The owners are moving to Texas to be near their daughter. I'm thinking about leasing the space."

"To expand the ice-cream business?"

"Expanding, yes, but it's not a lateral move, more of a branching out and complementing what I'm already doing." Maggie gave her daughter a sippy cup of water and the child eagerly grabbed it.

Emma did the same for Kyle. "I need a little more information if you want feedback. No pun intended."

She kept an eye on the diner behind her friend. The owners had just come out from the back and were involved in a conversation behind the counter.

"I'm thinking of adding food to the menu," Maggie said. "Sandwiches, maybe quiche. Soup and salad. Healthy choices."

"Something fast but nutritious," Emma guessed.

"Exactly. But I don't want to poach business from the diner. Michelle and Alan Crawford are friends."

Just then Wendy brought two cups and saucers and poured coffee in them from the pot she carried. "The menus are right there on the table when you're ready to order. Do you need cream?"

Both women nodded and she left again.

Emma picked up where her friend had left off. "I'd think both businesses are different. This is a sit-down-and-order place. More leisurely. You're talking about order, pick up and go, for people in a hurry."

"Exactly."

"I'd talk to the Caldwells." Technically she was a Caldwell, too, and she felt a sort of weird protectiveness for the people she barely knew.

"I planned to. But first I'm going to run it by Brady."

"Who?"

"My brother. Brady O'Keefe. He's the one in the family with business flair." Maggie was obviously proud of him. "He has an internet conglomerate that he runs remotely from his house. It's a really big house."

"Wow. He sounds like a very impressive guy."

"Hmm." Maggie tapped her lip, a speculative look in her eyes. "Speaking of setting people up…"

"Who was talking about setups?" Emma tried to look innocent.

"You. My brother is a bachelor. Never been married."

"And, to quote you, never falling in love means a lot less crying. God knows I've done enough."

"So that's how it is. Bad experience?"

"Like I said during the group, lying weasel dog." Emma figured she'd dodged a bullet there. "I've sworn off men."

"Okay. I understand. But if you ever want to talk—"

"No." Partly she just didn't want to reveal her stupidity, but mostly it was because Michelle was headed this way with an order pad in hand.

She stopped at the end of the table and looked at the children. "Hi, Danielle. Maggie, she's getting so big."

"Just turned one," the proud mother said. "Same age as Kyle."

"It's good to see you again, Emma. You, too, Mr. Kyle." She smiled at the babies. "Are these two little ones having their first date?"

"No," the two women said together with vehemence.

"Okay, then." Michelle laughed. "I am so sorry it took me such a long time to get over here."

"No problem. Emma and I have just been getting better acquainted."

"You're so sweet. We're short a waitress today. She had the flu and no one wants to be around that, including Alan and me. We told her to stay home and get better."

She glanced sympathetically at each of them. "But you must be starved."

"Don't worry about it." Emma had lost her appetite the moment Maggie suggested the diner. "The kids are happy. If they weren't, the crying would hit a decibel level that could be heard in the next county and you'd have begged us to leave."

"No," the other woman said teasingly. "That's not the best way to keep customers coming back."

"I guess not."

"So, what can I get you?"

Emma didn't need to look at the menu. "When Justin and I were here—"

"What?" Maggie stared at her. "This is news. You were here on a date?"

"It wasn't a date. We just had dinner—"

"Michelle, did you see this dinner?" Maggie was on a mission.

"I did."

"And?" The other woman studied the diner owner, then glanced at Emma. A curious expression slid into her eyes.

"It looked friendly enough." A diplomatic answer. "But not too friendly."

"Thank you," Emma said.

"I just noticed something." Maggie looked back and forth between them. Comparing. "Your eyes are almost exactly the same color."

Emma was just starting to relax, but now her heart jumped. "Really?"

"Yes. And the shape of your faces is very similar."

"You don't say?" The older woman looked more closely at Emma. "I consider that a compliment. You are so pretty and if Justin Flint doesn't see it, then he's not as smart as a doctor should be."

"Thank you again. I think." Emma wished she needed a menu. Maybe she could hide behind it. "You're short-handed. We should order. I think Kyle would like the Bear Cub combo. He loves macaroni and cheese. And just a Mama Bear burger for me."

"I'll have the same," Maggie said.

"Coming right up. And I'll bring a warm-up for those coffees."

When she was gone, Emma felt as if she could breathe again, trying to tell herself that this was no big deal. How many times had she been out with a friend and someone commented that they looked like sisters? That they must be related. What had just happened was the same thing, but she couldn't make herself believe the lie.

They *were* related.

Should she feel something for the woman? Her mother? The truth was, they were strangers. But how long before someone else noticed the resemblance and there was no way to blow it off?

Maybe this was the sign she'd been waiting for.

Justin watched Emma all through dinner, trying to figure out if she was upset or tired. Or both. She'd gone through the evening ritual of telling him about Kyle's day socializing and lunch at the Grizzly Bear Diner. Mentioning the restaurant her parents owned had made her mouth pull tight. If he had to put money on it, he'd bet something happened at lunch.

If he was smart, he'd mind his own business, but apparently he wasn't that bright, after all. He just couldn't stand the haunted look in her eyes.

After Kyle was tucked into his crib and sound asleep, it was her habit to putter in the kitchen. Before she went to her room, she got things ready for the Flints' morning rush. Everything was put together for breakfast except the food, and often she made a lunch for him to take to work. After turning off his computer in the office, that's where he found her now.

"Emma?"

She turned away from measuring grounds into a coffeemaker filter. "Hi. Is there something you need?"

You. The surge of yearning was startling in its intensity, but he was almost sure he didn't say that out loud. She looked so beautiful, so fragile and unhappy that he pushed his own feelings aside. More than he wanted her, he wanted to chase away whatever was troubling her.

"No," he said. "I don't need anything." He moved closer and leaned back against the island, sliding his fingers into the pockets of his jeans. A reminder to keep them to himself. "Do you want to talk about anything?"

Her gaze snapped to his and her hand froze. "Why would you think that? Did I do something wrong?"

"No, of course not. It's just you're not your usual perky self."

Justin had learned to watch his wife, read her mood, interpret when things were going her way and when to stay out of her way. He was pretty good at reading women, and mostly Emma had been easygoing—sweet, funny and sassy, which was why this pensive quality concerned him so much.

"What's bothering you?" he asked.

"It's not something that will affect my ability to care for Kyle. I'll handle it. Don't worry. It's not your responsibility. You're my boss."

"And your friend. At least I thought we were." They were something and it was a bad idea to define exactly what. Friends was the simplest label. "It might help to talk out whatever is going on."

She stared at him for several moments before the tension in her body eased with a slight nod. "Something happened at the diner today."

"Okay." He folded his arms over his chest. "Since there was no breaking news on the local TV station, you're going to have to give me a tiny bit more."

She thought for a moment, then said, "It's going to sound stupid when I say it out loud."

"I promise not to point and laugh."

"That doesn't make me feel better, but I sense you're not going to back off." She sighed. "Okay, here goes. Maggie Potter noticed that Michelle and I have some of the same physical characteristics. Face shape. Eye color."

"She said you look alike?"

"Not quite that direct. Just that there's a resemblance."

"She's your mother. If someone looks for it—"

"That's what bothers me," she said. "Maggie doesn't know. It was just an observation."

"Tell your mother the truth," he suggested.

"It's not that simple. They might hate me. What if they think I'm like the woman who took me?"

"Why would they?"

"I don't know," she said helplessly. "Maybe because my whole life is a lie."

"No, it's not."

"It feels that way. My fiancé cheated on me and I didn't know. That relationship was a lie. And my mother let me believe she gave birth to me when, in fact, she took me away from another woman." Her brown eyes were dark with the conflict raging inside her. "I can't bring myself to tell Michelle the truth, so doesn't that make me a product of my environment? A liar, too?"

"No." He rejected that categorically. "The woman who kidnapped you did a bad thing and we'll never know what desperation drove her to do it. But she didn't raise you to be a deceitful person. If that were the case, you wouldn't have told me the truth after I hired you. None of this is your fault."

"Not the situation, but I'm certainly responsible for what's going on now. And I was wrong. It is affecting my work performance."

"No, it's not." His son was happy and healthy. His household ran like a well-oiled machine. She did her job superbly. She wasn't to blame for the fact that he couldn't stop thinking about her in his bed.

"Don't you see? If I was doing my job well, you'd never have known there was something bothering me. I'm normally a better nanny than this." Her eyes filled with what looked like pity directed at him. "You ought to have someone stronger, someone better. Especially after losing your wife."

"Don't," he snapped.

"What?"

Justin was sick of holding this inside and couldn't do it anymore. "Don't pity me. I don't deserve it."

"I'm not. I don't feel sorry for you. It's just—"

"Nothing. Don't say it," he pleaded.

"I have to." Her small smile was sad around the edges. "You lost the love of your life. A lot of people would have been immobilized by something like that, but you weren't. You moved forward. You relocated to Blackwater Lake, a place where her memory wouldn't get you down."

"I came here so Kyle could have a normal, well-balanced life."

"Where he wouldn't miss his mother as much because people didn't know her," she protested.

"Unfortunately, my past followed me."

"What do you mean?"

"People knew my story and treated me like the lonely widower—" He dragged his fingers through his hair. "I can't stand it anymore. I can't stand living the lie."

"You're scaring me, Justin." She folded her arms across her waist. "What are you talking about?"

"I didn't love my wife. I wouldn't have wished her dead because no matter her flaws, she was Kyle's mother. Whatever she was, he needed her in his life and her being gone will always make him wonder what might have been. But when she died, we were separated. I'd asked her for a divorce. We both knew there was nothing between us anymore."

She looked surprised but not disapproving. "No one knows this?"

"At first I didn't want to talk about it. I wanted to forget and thought it would blow over, but somehow my previous life has become mysterious and intriguing. It was just easier to let them go on believing than to confess the truth. What could it hurt? She's gone." He didn't see anything in Emma's expression that hinted at her despising him. That was a plus. "After she was involved in that fatal car accident, it was the first and only time I was grateful that she'd ignored her child."

"She turned her back on her baby?"

"All the time. Even when he wasn't feeling well. Heaven forbid she'd miss a social thing. She'd still go to formal events, turning him over to me or the nanny. She walked out without looking back." The memory made him angry all over again. "It drove me nuts how she could do that. Finally I realized that I didn't much like the woman I married."

Understanding dawned in Emma's eyes. "You were grateful she ignored Kyle because he wasn't in the car with her when she had the accident."

"Yes." He met her gaze because now that he was finally coming clean it was important that she fully understood how low he could go. "So, you're not the only one living a lie. I'm not the man everyone thinks."

"That's your private past and no one's business but yours. You're a good man. Never doubt that."

He wasn't so sure. "It's hard not to."

"Oh, Justin—" She moved close and put her arms around him. "I've never seen someone who needs a hug more than you do right now."

He had every intention of pushing her away. He really did. But the nearness of her body, the exquisite feel of her soft curves pressed against him were too much temptation after weeks of denying himself. Last night in the pumpkin patch when they'd held each other was never far from his mind. The feminine weight of her in his arms haunted his dreams and he wasn't completely convinced that right this moment wasn't another dream.

So he held her close for several moments and sighed, a ragged shuddering sound, because touching her overwhelmed his willpower.

"Emma—" Her name was a sigh on his lips as he cupped her cheek in his hand and lowered his mouth to hers.

A moan of acceptance caught in her throat and the sound set his blood on fire. His brain shut down as his senses kicked into overdrive. He kissed her slowly, thoroughly, concentrating on the feel of her full lips, the cadence of her quickened breathing, the silky hair that tickled his fingers.

He wanted more. The idea of carrying her to his room had far too much appeal and he ached to do just that. But some part of his sensation-drugged brain managed to sputter to life and convey the message that this wasn't a good idea.

"Emma—" Justin pulled back, breathing hard. "I'm sorry. That was out of line."

She met his gaze, her own breathing unsteady, her eyes full of wonder. "It was just a kiss."

"That's where you're wrong." He cupped her face in both hands now, unable to stop touching her. "I want more than just a kiss and we should stop right now."

Her voice was husky, her expression full of sass and searing need when she said, "Maybe we shouldn't."

Chapter Eight

"One of us has to be strong." The words were right, but there was no conviction in Justin's voice. "Do we really want to take this step?"

Emma couldn't speak for him, but *she* desperately wanted to. When he'd confessed to not being in love with the wife he'd lost, her reservations had disappeared. Or it could be the way he'd kissed her had chased away her will to resist. Either way, she couldn't rally the enthusiasm to be the strong one here.

"Emma..." He brushed his thumb gently over her cheek as his eyes searched hers. "You're so sweet—"

His hesitation took the air out of her brazen balloon. She'd jumped to a conclusion and it was wrong. He didn't want her and, dear God, this was humiliating on so many levels.

She stepped away from him, incapable of thinking rationally when he was touching her. That much was obvious because apparently she'd been under the impression that if she let him know how she felt, he would want her, too.

"This was obviously a mistake. I'll just be going. Good

night, Justin." She turned, prepared to head upstairs as fast as possible.

He put a hand on her arm. "Wait—"

Without looking at him, she shook her head. "You're right. We have to be strong—"

"No."

She heard the grinding need in his frustrated tone and gratefully turned into his arms, then slid her own around his waist. "I thought I was the only one who felt this way. I thought—"

"You'd be wrong." He kissed her mouth softly, a peck and a promise. "I felt something the first time I saw you. When you came to my office at the clinic."

"Really?"

He nodded. "I had an idea in my head of the nanny I was looking for and you're not it. Except that you're a natural with my son."

"Oh? What was your vision?"

"Old. Gray. Plump. A wart on the end of your nose would have been an excellent qualification."

"And you hired me, anyway."

"Your work history and recommendations were impeccable." He shrugged. "And I was so sure the attraction would go away. Wow, was I wrong about that."

He wasn't the only one, she thought. "I know exactly what you mean."

"Emma?"

She left her hands at his waist and looked up at him. "What?"

"I'm taking you to bed now."

"Yes." She picked up the baby monitor beside her on the counter then slid her free hand into his.

Justin took her through the family room to the hall that led to the first-floor master bedroom. It was a suite, really, large and masculine, decorated in shades of brown, beige and black. The furniture was pine and so right for this house with its spectacular views of tree-covered mountains.

Obviously Emma had seen it, what with putting away laundry and replacing towels in the attached bath. But she'd never *seen* it from the perspective of being in the big, soft king-size bed with Justin. She'd fought so hard against this, but apparently it was true what they said about the wanting being bigger than both of them. The present was clear as a bell, but the future wasn't. She refused to think about that right now and set the baby monitor on one of the nightstands by the bed, then turned to Justin.

Light from the hall trickled over his face as they stood beside the high mattress. Gray eyes stormy and intense, he reached for the hem of her sweater and lifted it up and off. She slowly unbuttoned his shirt, then spread it wide, sliding the cotton from his broad shoulders.

With their gazes locked, she reached behind her back to unhook her bra, letting it fall to the carpet at their feet on the growing pile of discarded clothing. Justin's breath caught as he slowly reached out and gently took her left breast in his hand, rubbing the tip with his thumb.

"I honestly can't believe how beautiful you are," he whispered reverently.

"You make me feel that way." Her heartbeat went wild as he caressed her bare, sensitive skin. Tingles two-stepped up and down her arms.

Without looking away, he reached for the buckle on his belt and unfastened it before flicking open the button on his jeans. After toeing off his shoes, he slid the zipper south and pushed off pants and briefs.

Emma removed her own sneakers and skimmed off everything until she was naked, too. Along with their clothes, it felt as if all pretense and secrets had been stripped away. They were simply a woman and a man who wanted each other. There were no barriers between them; this intimacy was honest.

Justin pulled her into his arms, skin to skin. He kissed her tenderly and left her needing so much more. But when he looked into her eyes, he put into words exactly what she'd been feeling.

"This is the first thing that feels real to me in a very long time."

"I know what you mean."

He let her go long enough to toss throw pillows aside and drag the comforter down, leaving the sheets bare. Then he took her in his arms again and held her tight against him while lowering them together onto the thick mattress.

His mouth took hers slowly, thoroughly, and when her lips parted, his tongue slid inside to explore the interior with just as much attention. On their sides facing each other, they nibbled and nipped, quick drugging kisses as his hand skimmed the curve of her waist. Moving first up to the side of her breast, his fingers stroked and touched until she could hardly stand the pressure building inside her. Then he slid his hand over her belly and lower, fingers hovering, teasing while her tension surged.

Emma drifted on a sea of sensation, each wave cresting until the next, larger swell took her breath away again. She let her hands roam freely, restless strokes up to his broad shoulders and down over the wide contour of his chest. When her palm brushed his nipple, he hissed out a sharp sound of arousal.

Each moment was like a bright fluffy cloud pushed by the wind across the sky before she could absorb the magnificence. She wanted to hold on to everything, keep each second close to her heart forever.

Then rational thought vanished completely as he touched a finger to the place at the juncture of her thighs where nerve endings came together. The sensation had her gasping against his lips and nearly brought her up off the mattress. Justin was panting with fractured breaths as he reached into the nightstand.

"What?"

"Condom—"

She nodded, unable to say anything else, grateful that he'd thought about it because she hadn't. In seconds he'd ripped open the package and put on the protection. She rolled to her back as he levered himself over her, gently urging her legs wide with his knee. Then he braced on his forearms and slowly nudged inside, letting her grow accustomed to the feel of him, the thickness.

Emma turned her face into the masculine swell of his biceps and breathed in the tantalizing spicy scent of his skin. He moved inside her, stoking the knot of tension tighter and tighter until she came apart in a glorious explosion. He held her tenderly, kissed her forehead, cheek and hair, as pleasure rippled through her. When she could finally think again, she lifted her hips, urging him on until he went still and groaned out his own release.

"Oh, God, Emma. Not yet—" He buried his face in her neck.

She held him for a long time, something scratching at her thoughts, warning not to let go.

Not yet.

Finally, Justin rolled away and without a word got out of bed. Dimly she was aware of a light switching on, but she didn't open her eyes.

In the darkness of burned-out passion, Emma could feel unease creeping in. Then the mattress dipped and Justin pulled her against his side. But she felt the difference, a distance, a reluctance. There was tension in his arms now where before he hadn't been able to hold her close enough.

She'd managed to turn off her head because touching and being touched had felt too good to stop. It was two people doing what they wanted in all the right ways. Now all the ways it was wrong couldn't be silenced. Just enough time had passed for the magnitude of what they'd done to penetrate the afterglow of lovemaking. Rules and regrets came rushing in.

"Justin, I'm sorry—"

"I'm not," he said fiercely. "It's just—"

She knew. "It can't happen again. I'm the nanny and you're my employer."

"If that was all, I would just fire you." There was anger and frustration in his voice. The words implied he had different reasons for backing off.

"Maybe you *should* let me go." She'd find another job. Something to get by until she resolved her situation.

"It's not that simple." He rolled onto his side toward her. "I just don't want you to get the wrong idea."

"About what?" She pulled the sheet up more snugly, as if it could protect her from what was coming.

"We want different things. You're looking for family and mine is already complete. I have Kyle and he's all I want. I have no intention of ever marrying again. Nothing has changed for me."

Hearing that he hadn't liked his wife very much had freed her to make love with him, but the pain of what he'd gone through locked her out now. His words from the first job interview came back to her.

I'm not looking for a wife.

The thing was, he was right to say that. She wanted honesty and he'd been that way right from the beginning. Besides, her life was too complicated already. If they pulled back now, this was nothing more than momentary weakness. No harm, no foul.

"I understand, Justin. And you're absolutely right. We'll forget this ever happened."

"Okay," he answered with genuine regret. "That would be best."

There was a snuffling sound from the baby monitor followed by a whimper. Bless that baby boy who spared her from having to say more.

"I need to check on Kyle."

From now on, she would keep busy with the baby and try not to wonder how she was going to keep the promise she'd just made to his father.

Forget this ever happened? Fat chance.

"You had sex."

Justin had no idea how Camille Halliday knew, but he didn't plan to comment on her declaration. Instead, he pointed at her pregnant tummy and made a declaration of his own. "Someone certainly did."

"Yes, but I'm in a relationship. And you didn't deny it."

He looked around the hallway to make sure no one in the clinic had heard what she said. "Do you enjoy being outrageous?"

The question was a deflection, mostly because he didn't want to ask how she'd guessed. The guilt was probably there in his eyes; he was the scumbag boss. Creating a hostile work environment. Although what they did felt anything but hostile. Maybe he should start a new reality show about sleazy employers who slept with the staff. Except she'd been so warm and willing in his arms.

"I used to enjoy being outrageous when I was young and a mixed-up kid." Cam settled her hands on her pregnant belly. "Now I've reformed and have a kid of my own on the way. And, I say again, you didn't deny having sex."

Another deflection was needed since she was calling him out. "What are you doing here?"

"I had a doctor's appointment. The baby and I are in very good health and all is progressing normally, Adam says."

Adam Stone was Mercy Medical Clinic's family practice physician and took care of the pregnant patients. Justin liked and respected him.

"So if you've seen Adam, how come you're still here?" Bugging me, he wanted to add.

"I'm waiting for Ben. He's taking me out to lunch."

"So where is he?"

Justin could really use some help here, because he didn't particularly want to talk about Emma. They'd said everything there was to say in his bed last night, just before she'd gone upstairs to the baby. This morning she'd made an effort at normal and so had he, but tension was on the menu right along with his omelet.

"My gorgeous fiancé is with a patient. What are you doing right now?"

He slid his hands into the pockets of his white lab coat. "I'm on my way to the break room for lunch."

"Good. I'll keep you company." She put her arm through his and tugged him down the hall, past patient rooms to the last door on the left.

Inside, there was a refrigerator, stainless-steel sink and cupboards. A card table and four folding chairs dominated the center of the room. At one time this area was used for storage as well as a place for employees to take a break. But since the clinic expansion, there was a much larger room designated for storing supplies and equipment.

Camille looked around, an odd expression in her pretty blue eyes.

"What?"

"It just now hit me. This sure is different from your Beverly Hills office."

"I know."

"Do you miss it? Do you ever regret moving here?" she asked.

"No," he said instantly.

"Take your time. Think about it."

"I don't have to. The longer I live here in Blackwater Lake, the more convinced I am that moving from Beverly Hills was the right decision. Blackwater is a close-knit community made up of down-to-earth people. It's the ideal place for Kyle to grow up."

"So, you have doubts," she teased.

"Right." He grinned, then opened the refrigerator and took out the brown bag Emma had packed his lunch in.

A vision of her in his bed, silky brown hair spread over his pillow, was like a sucker punch to the gut. It had been one of the best nights of his life. And the worst. Any doubts he had weren't about what they'd done but were directed at himself. He'd let down his guard and couldn't take back having sex with her. His punishment was that he continued to want her even though he couldn't have her.

He sat in one of the chairs and pulled out the chicken sandwich but suddenly wasn't hungry, at least not for food.

Camille tapped her lip, studying him. "You've got that look again."

"What look would that be?" he asked with as much innocence as he could, what with the guilt he was carrying.

"You had sex. With Emma."

He was just lifting half the sandwich to his mouth and

froze. A couple seconds later and he'd have taken a bite, probably choked on it.

"Seriously, Cam. You think I'm that low?" He was, but she didn't know it for a fact.

"I think you're that attracted to your nanny. And who could blame you?" She took a bottle of water from the fridge and sat at a right angle to him. "She's beautiful, Justin. Inside and out. Kyle adores her."

"She's good with him," he agreed.

"And you." She tucked a strand of blond hair behind her ear then folded her hands around the plastic bottle. "You look different. More relaxed, or something."

"Or something."

He sure didn't feel in control. If anything, he was even more tense. Having Emma was even better than he'd imagined and his imagination was pretty good.

"Oh, for Pete's sake." Cam's voice was full of friendly frustration. "Are you afraid I'll spread stories around town?"

"It never crossed my mind," he said truthfully. "But why do you want to know?"

"Female curiosity. And a sincere hope for you to be happy."

"That's sweet." If he'd had a sister, he would want her to be just like Camille Halliday. Funny, abrasive, straightforward and sympathetic.

"All right, then. Just admit it. This is me. I've been victimized by gossip and rumors for as long as I can remember. Do you really think I'd spread around something so personal, something you shared with me privately? As a friend?"

"No." The truth was, he could use someone to talk to. "That's one lucky kid you've got there. You're going to be a great mom."

She smiled with pleasure. "How do you know?"

"Because that child won't be able to get away with anything. You're very discerning." He took a big bite of chicken salad on wheat. It was every bit as good as Emma always made it. The thought of her made his body grow tight with need and a hunger that had nothing to do with food.

"It was actually just a guess, but now you've pretty much confirmed that you had sex with Emma."

"Just out of curiosity, how did you know it was her?"

"She's living under your roof. You haven't been seeing anyone else or I'd have heard about it. And I saw the way you looked at her when Ben and I were there for Kyle's birthday." She shrugged. "Easy."

"Hmm." He took another bite of his sandwich.

"So why don't you look happier?"

"It's not going to happen again."

"Yes, it is," she insisted.

"No."

"Why not?" Her eyes narrowed. "She's not trying to pull a fast one, is she?"

"No way." Justin was surprised by how quickly and aggressively he defended Emma. "You're too cynical."

"With good reason." She twisted the top off her water bottle. "But if you two have the hots for each other, I don't understand how you can back off."

"We're in agreement about it." He couldn't speak for Emma, but it was the hardest damn thing he'd ever done. "There's baggage. On both sides."

He looked at the other half of his sandwich, cut like a triangle. Such a little gesture that kept it from being ordinary. Probably didn't take any more time, but was just one more thing that Em did for him. Unlike Kristina. The woman he'd been stupid enough to marry had only ever thought of herself.

"You met my wife," he said to Cam. "You know the marriage was an unqualified disaster."

She nodded. "I was always surprised that you married someone so shallow and self-centered. You're such a good man and she didn't deserve you."

"I fell hard and fast for who I thought she was." He shrugged. "I didn't know she was putting on an act."

"She'd made up her mind that she wanted to be married to a renowned Beverly Hills plastic surgeon and pulled out all the stops to get him."

"If you knew, why didn't you warn me?"

"A—you wouldn't have believed me. And B—I didn't know you very well back then. I'm sorry."

"You didn't force me to propose."

She took a sip of water. "But you got a perfect little boy out of it. And you have to think about him."

"He's all I am thinking about. The worst thing I could do is burden Kyle with another mistake. My bad judgment is the best reason not to get serious again."

"Well, I'm a good judge of character and in my humble opinion Emma is the real deal."

"But what if you're wrong? What if she's not?" He dragged his fingers through his hair. "I won't take another chance, and it would be really wrong to lead her on when I have no intention of getting serious."

"But, Justin—"

He held up a hand. "Not going to happen, Cam."

"Okay. You're wrong to deny yourself happiness, but I think you'll get over it in time, with someone willing to be patient with you." She smiled at the pun. "But I'll get off your back for right now."

"Thank you."

"So, that witch of a wife is your baggage. What about Emma? What's hers?"

Justin couldn't tell her that. Emma had confided in him and he wouldn't betray her trust. The question was how to get the message to this sharp, curious woman without letting anything slip. "Cam, it's not for me to—"

"Dr. Flint?"

He looked at the doorway where the nurse stood. "Hi, Ginny. What's up?"

"You have an emergency walk-in. Alan Crawford, from the Grizzly Bear Diner. A grease burn. Room one."

He nodded. "I'll be right there."

"Michelle, his wife, is with him and she's filling out paperwork."

"Okay." The nurse disappeared and he looked at Cam. "Gotta go."

"Of course. I hope it's not too serious."

"Me, too."

"But if there's anything good about this, it's that he's got you for his doctor." Cam smiled her encouragement. "Bye, Justin."

Speaking of Emma's baggage, he was on his way to see them.

Chapter Nine

Justin headed down the hall toward room one where Emma's father waited. If the man had walked himself into the clinic, chances were good the injury wasn't too serious. Hopefully, that was the case because the last thing she needed was more conflict.

He stopped at the closed door and took the chart from the plastic holder on the wall. Voices, one male the other female, drifted to him as he flipped through the pages and scanned Mr. Crawford's medical history. Adam Stone's notes indicated he had regular physicals and was a generally healthy man who exercised and took care of himself.

He knocked once on the door and heard a deep voice say, "Come in."

Alan was sitting on the exam table, a wet white towel draped over his left forearm. He was wearing a short-sleeved green-collared shirt with an embroidered grizzly bear on the left front. His worn blue jeans showed dark splotches that could be oil, but it didn't appear that any clothing had adhered to the wound.

"Hi, Justin."

"Alan. I'd shake your hand and ask how you are, but rumor has it there was an accident."

"Hot grease." Michelle's chin quivered as she stood beside her husband, worry evident in her eyes.

A feature that she'd passed on to Emma. No wonder Maggie had noticed the resemblance. He was surprised he hadn't seen it before. Probably because he hadn't been looking for it. Now he saw the similarity in the curve of her cheek, lip and brow lines, the shape of the forehead. And their eyes were the same warm shade of brown shot with specks of gold. She was still a very attractive woman and in twenty-five or thirty years this is what Emma would look like.

"Justin?" Alan's voice was a mixture of pain-laced tension with a dash of teasing. "Should I be worried?"

"Sorry, Alan." Justin pushed all thoughts aside and focused his concentration on the patient. "Let's take a look and see what we've got."

After sliding on a pair of disposable gloves, Justin lifted the towel to look at the wound. The area from just above the wrist almost to the elbow was bright red. So far there was no blistering and he gently touched the area. The patient hissed out a breath.

"Sorry." Justin met the other man's gaze. "Believe it or not, pain is a good sign."

"Oh?" Beads of perspiration popped out on the other man's forehead. "Obviously I'm still breathing, but on every other level it just plain sucks."

"Pain is an indicator that it's a second-degree burn and only two layers of skin are affected. No pain would mean that it's third-degree trauma and all layers of skin destroyed. That type of injury can't heal without surgical intervention and recovery is more than twice as long. Scarring is usually severe."

"So I'm lucky." He smiled at his wife, who nodded.

"I'll need to reevaluate this in a couple of days to make sure, but all signs point to you being very fortunate."

"If it turns out to be more severe," Michelle asked, "what's involved in surgery?"

"I'd need to debride the burn—that means remove the dead skin. Then apply a graft."

"From Alan's skin?" she asked.

"That's right. We take it from the buttocks or inner thigh, somewhere it's not noticeable. Then it's applied to the open wound as a covering and held in place by a dressing and a few stitches. All of that is done under general anesthesia because, honestly, it's a painful procedure. But that's worst-case scenario. We're not there yet. And I don't think surgery will be necessary if the burn is taken care of now."

"Then I guess pain *is* good."

"It's annoying," Justin agreed. "But always a good idea to pay attention."

"In the meantime, what's the treatment?" Alan asked.

"Skin is the largest organ in the body and the first line of defense when there's an injury. But infection is a major risk with injuries like this. Many medications are hard to use with burns. Some cause pain. Others are effective only against a narrow range of bacteria." Justin met his gaze. "So, I'm going to clean it up with Betadine, then apply a coating of silver sulfadiazine cream. It doesn't initiate pain and should knock down most bacteria. It lets the body devote all energy to healing instead of depleting reserves to fight infection."

Alan nodded at his wife. "Probably a good thing you bullied me into coming to the clinic."

"I'd say so." She looked at Justin. "He kept insisting ice water and lavender were just what the doctor ordered."

"And she demanded to know if I'd bought a medical degree online," her husband teased.

Justin laughed. "The internet is full of information, but not all of it is accurate. When in doubt consult a health care professional."

"We're lucky to have you in Blackwater Lake, Doc."

"It's a great place to live and I'm happy to be a part of this community and Mercy Medical Clinic." He took a prescription pad from his lab coat pocket and started to write on it. "This is the cream and I want you to put it on twice a day. Keep the affected area covered with nonstick pads and gauze to hold it there. I've given you several re-fills, and if you need more just have the pharmacy call for an authorization."

Michelle took the paper from him and put it in her purse. "Thank you, Justin."

"For now, I'll clean and dress the wound."

"That's going to hurt, right, Doc?" Alan glanced at his wife.

Justin nodded sympathetically. "I believe in telling the truth. It will smart, but I'll be quick."

Michelle looked at her husband with the same concerned expression that Emma sometimes wore. "I'll stay if you want."

"She can't stand to see someone she loves in pain," Alan explained. "With our boys there were always stitches, scrapes and even a broken bone once."

"I felt like the world's worst mother when Alan held their hand through the treatment." She sighed. "We both agreed that was probably better than me passing out or getting sick in front of them."

"You're an amazing mother," her husband defended. "And we're a team. What I did was easy. You kept the rest of the family calm and on a steady course. That was hard."

Justin could see their family dynamic at work. It's how they'd gotten through the trauma of their daughter's abduction. The divorce rate was very high in situations like that, but Emma's parents beat the odds. She came from strong and resilient roots. He just wished he could make her see that deep character she'd inherited would get her through.

"So, you're going to be in the waiting room, honey?"

Michelle nodded. "If he passes out, you know where to find me, Justin."

"I'll be fine." Alan leaned over and kissed her quickly. "Don't worry."

"Yeah, that'll happen." She opened the door and stepped out, then closed it behind her.

"I thought she'd never leave."

"Excuse me?" Justin stared at him.

"Look, Doc, you get the hard part done, then we'll talk. There's something I want to ask you."

Justin didn't get the feeling it was about anything serious. In spite of the no-doubt-painful burn he'd suffered, Alan Crawford was excited and had clearly wanted his wife out of the room for some reason.

After retrieving a basin from the cupboard above the sink, Justin handed it to the patient. "Hold your arm over that. I'm going to disinfect the wound."

"Okay. I'm bracing myself."

Justin worked quickly to wash the burned area. Then he took the sterile pad and smeared it with silver sulfadiazine cream, placing the compress over the affected area before winding white gauze around the arm to hold the covering in place.

"That wasn't too bad, Doc."

"Good. A tip for changing the dressing. It's easier on you if the cream goes on the pad first."

"I'll pass that information onto my wife."

"If necessary, try over-the-counter medications for pain. But if that doesn't help, call me and I can prescribe something to make you comfortable."

"Will do."

"Okay," Justin said. "So, what did you want to ask?"

"I'm having a birthday party for Michelle." He grinned. "She's turning fifty-five. I didn't get my act together when she was fifty and she won't be expecting this until the next milestone at sixty. So I think I can pull off a surprise with this one."

"Sounds reasonable." Justin wasn't sure why he was sharing this.

"I want you to come."

"Me?" He slid his hands into his lab coat pockets. "Why?"

"She likes you." He shrugged. "Go figure."

"Thanks, I think."

"Seriously, the invitation is for the whole clinic staff and I'd be grateful if you could extend it to everyone for me. That way, Michelle won't catch on. It will be tricky enough to have it at the house without her getting suspicious, but I'll figure out something."

Justin folded his arms over his chest. "I don't know what to say."

"Say you'll be there. And bring someone. Michelle would call it your plus one, and if you don't have anyone with you, it's pretty much a sure thing that she'll fix you up. So if you know what's good for you..."

"I don't really know anyone to ask." Emma popped into his mind, but that probably wasn't a good idea.

"I'm sure there are a lot of ladies in Blackwater Lake who would like to change that. But if you want my advice, you should invite that pretty nanny of yours." He held up his good hand to stop a protest. "I saw you two at dinner in the diner. Seemed like you were getting along fine."

They had been, Justin remembered. But that was before he'd taken her to bed. "I don't know..."

"Call it a job perk for her. She's with the baby all day and sure seems to love what she does, but I'm sure she'd enjoy an evening out. Michelle sure did when we had four little ones."

Justin saw the dark look in his patient's eyes for just a moment and knew what he was thinking. "I know about your daughter being taken. I don't mean to pry—"

"I know. The thing is, sometimes I need to talk about her." Alan sighed, his good hand fisted on his thigh. "In our hearts we never moved on from the baby we lost, but for the sake of our sons, we couldn't stand still."

"That took a lot of courage."

The man shook his head. "It was all we could do. The cops told us there was probably no chance that she was still alive, but we think about her every day and hold out hope that she'll come home. There are stories on the news with happy endings. It happens."

"That's true," Justin said. He could feel this man's emotional pain and was deeply tempted to tell him the truth. But it wasn't his truth to tell.

Alan met his gaze. "Closure is something of a cliché, but only people who go through what we did can understand why it's precious. We'd just like to know what happened to our baby girl."

Justin simply nodded. There was nothing he could say that wouldn't betray Emma's confidence.

The other man blew out a long breath, then slid off the exam table. "Michelle and I really like you. I hope you'll come to the party. Bring Emma and Kyle, too. We think the world of that little guy."

He is my *world,* Justin thought. Just as Emma would have been for her parents. This party might be just the thing to put her mind at ease. All he had to do was figure out how to convince her to go.

"Knock, knock."

With a very sleepy Kyle in her arms, Emma stood just outside Justin's office and rapped lightly on the door frame. The baby tried to imitate her and slapped at the molding. He was growing so fast, getting big and heavy. He was all little boy in his footie pajamas and ready for bed.

His father smiled. "Come in. The door is always open."

"Literally," she teased. "Seriously, you never close your door. And this little boy can get pretty loud and rambunctious." She hugged the baby and nuzzled his neck until he laughed.

"It seems like the paperwork never ends. There are charts to update and procedures to study. I like to plan and be prepared before a surgery."

"Patients like that in a doctor."

He laughed. "But I always want Kyle to feel he can come in if he wants. For any reason."

"Even if it's to take this new walking thing out for a spin?" She set the boy down on his feet and steadied him before letting go. "I told him it was time for bed and he made a break for it. I grabbed him up just outside your door."

"Were you coming to say good-night, pal?" As the boy rounded the corner of the desk, Justin picked him up and held him close for a moment.

The sight of the strong man holding his child and the love shining in those intense gray eyes never failed to trip up Emma's heart. Justin Flint was capable of such deep emotion, and any woman fortunate enough to win his affection would be extraordinarily lucky. She knew he wasn't willing to take a chance now, but maybe someday a woman would come along to chase away enough of the bad memories for him to try again. Emma also knew she wasn't that woman.

The sex had been amazing and if he were a less principled man it would have happened again. She ached from wanting him, but he was too ethical and honest to promise what he couldn't give. The morning after had been awkward, but they'd both pretended to ignore what happened and the uneasiness passed. He was friendly, a little reserved, but that was to be expected. Emma was doing her best to follow his lead. He would never know her feelings for him had grown stronger.

Justin was talking quietly to the toddler, who was doing his level best to get at the computer, paperwork and other office paraphernalia that were too tempting to a little boy.

He looked at her. "I'm not sure whether or not to be proud that he doesn't give up."

"Repeat this ten times. Determination is a good quality in an adult."

"Meaning, not so much in a one-year-old."

"You got it. Also keep in mind that this stage doesn't last forever. He'll learn what's okay and what's not."

Kyle almost got his little hands on the stapler, and Justin stood up so everything was out of reach. "And that's something not okay. I shudder to think what staples would do if he swallowed them."

"It's my job to make sure that doesn't happen," she said.

No one could take better care of him than her, Emma realized. That wasn't ego talking. It wasn't about the job. It was love, pure and simple.

When Kyle couldn't get to what he was after, he let out a loud wail and began to rub his eyes. Then he leaned toward her and tried to wriggle out of his father's arms. Good luck with that, she thought. The man had that devastating combination of strength and tenderness that would have women throwing their panties at him if he were a rock star.

Kyle cried again and she moved closer to take him, trying to ignore the sparking sensation when her hands brushed Justin's.

"Okay, kiddo. I know you're tired. Time to go night-night." The toddler's nose was running and she fished a tissue from her jeans pocket to wipe it. Then she turned so Kyle could see his father. "Tell Daddy good-night."

Because she was facing away from him, Justin couldn't see the yearning she knew would be in her eyes. But she could feel the warmth from his body when he moved in behind her and kissed his son's forehead.

"Sleep tight, pal."

Maybe it was wishful thinking, but she would swear he was breathing just a little unsteadily and his voice was this side of smoky. Whether or not that impression was fueled by imagination, her body responded and liquid heat poured through her. When Kyle was in his crib, she could stay upstairs. All things considered, she was better off with a flight of stairs between them.

When father and son had said their good-nights, she started for the door, grateful to get some distance.

"Emma?"

She half turned toward him. "Yes?"

"When Kyle is settled for the night, would you mind coming back down? There's something I'd like to talk to you about."

"Of course."

He looked serious and she wondered if this was where he gave notice that the situation wasn't working for him. Her stomach dropped at the thought of leaving Kyle. And

Justin. She wasn't sure which one of them she would miss more and knew they were a package deal.

She walked up the stairs and Kyle seemed to get heavier in her arms as he relaxed into sleep. Normally she rocked him in the glider for a few minutes, but he was practically out now. Pressing her lips to his forehead, she decided he didn't feel too warm, but the runny nose and cranky disposition were out of character for him. She hoped he wasn't getting sick.

Emma put him on his back in the crib and covered him with a light blanket. "Good night, little man. Sleep well."

She turned on the night-light, picked up the baby monitor and tiptoed from the nursery and down the stairs. Prepared to meet Justin in his office, she was surprised to see him sitting in the family room. She wasn't sure what to make of that, figuring he'd wanted to discuss her continued employment, and the office was best for that kind of conversation.

She walked over to the sofa and set the monitor on the coffee table without sitting down. "So what did you want to talk about?"

"I saw Alan Crawford today at the clinic."

Several things raced through her mind. Did Alan know something about her? Or was he at Mercy Medical Clinic because of a health issue? It surprised her that she felt anxious about a man she barely knew.

"Is he all right?" she finally asked.

Justin nodded. "An accident at the diner. He'll be fine."

She wanted to fire questions at him, the way she'd done with her mother's doctor after the breast cancer recurred. But she didn't have the same relationship with her biological father. And how messed up was that?

"I know I can't ask you for details on his condition because of privacy issues. That would put you in an awkward position."

Justin nodded. "But you could ask him yourself."

"I can't do that." She shook her head. "No way can I march up to the counter at the diner and say, 'So you saw the doctor. Care to share?'"

"You don't have to go to the diner," he said mysteriously.

"What do you mean?"

"Alan is having a surprise fifty-fifth birthday party for his wife."

It was noteworthy that he didn't say the get-together was for her mother. Emma appreciated his sensitivity. "That's really sweet of him, but I'm not sure what that has to do with me."

"I was invited and he suggested you come along."

"Why?" Did this mean he wasn't terminating her employment? Suddenly, sitting down seemed like an awesome idea, so she did. She was at a right angle to him on the full-size sofa.

"He said you probably needed a night out and remembered that Michelle appreciated it when they had four small kids."

"Four? But there are three... Oh," she said when his meaning sank in.

"Yeah." He rested his elbows on his knees.

"Why did he ask you?"

"Actually, he invited the whole staff at the clinic. To put a finer point on it, he asked me to invite the staff because he couldn't figure out how to do it without spilling the secret to his wife. I got the feeling he's pretty much inviting most of Blackwater Lake. He said the diner is closing down for the evening so their staff can attend, but the gathering will be at their home."

"I see." No, she didn't. "It's really nice of him to think of me, but it's probably not a good idea."

"For whom?" His question was direct and challenging.

Instead of answering him immediately, she made a lateral move. "Who's going to take care of Kyle? I can't leave him."

"Alan said we should bring him. Other people are bringing their kids along." He straightened and leaned back against the sofa. "This would be a good opportunity for you to get to know your family."

"You're probably right about that," she agreed. "But I'm not sure about telling them who I am. It doesn't seem right to put them through all that emotional upheaval when they seem okay."

Part of her actually believed that. The other part figured fear was holding her back. Fear of rejection followed by having to move on with her life. Moving on might mean leaving town and she was selfish enough to want this time with Justin to go on just a little longer.

"You need to know something, Emma." He blew out a long breath. "It might appear that they're okay, but I still saw the pain in Alan's eyes. He told me they went forward for the sake of their sons. People have to move on when something bad happens."

"You didn't," she pointed out, not sure why the words tumbled out of her mouth.

His eyes darkened, but his voice was calm when he answered. "My situation was different. I moved on emotionally before my wife died. Not wanting to make another mistake isn't the same as living in the past."

Maybe not, but that distinction didn't make much difference to the present. It was just wrong that a man so capable of great love would be alone by choice. The realization made her angry at the woman who'd done this to him.

"I'm sorry. It's none of my business." Although that didn't keep her from having an opinion.

"Don't worry about it." He met her gaze and something hot slid into his before he said, "The thing is, I have another reason for wanting you there."

"Oh?"

"Alan warned me that if I'm alone, his wife will do her best to fix me up with someone at the party."

"I see." She couldn't help smiling now. "So, this is all about you."

"Of course."

"You're not worried that we might be the focus of town hearsay, grist for the gossip mill if we're seen at a big party together?"

"Nope? You?" Again he was issuing a challenge.

She decided not to share the fact that because they lived under the same roof they were already rumor central with the moms at Kyle's play group. Emma figured that was a pretty good sampling of what was being said all over Blackwater Lake.

It was clear that for his own reasons he wanted her to go with him to this gathering. And when he'd first asked, she'd had every intention of turning him down, even though it was a very good opportunity to interact with her parents, not to mention her brothers. Oddly enough, it was the matchmaking thing her father had probably said in jest that changed her mind.

For the record, jealousy was a powerful motivator.

"All right, Justin. You've made your point. I'll go with you to the party."

Chapter Ten

The next morning, the party several weeks away was the last thing on Emma's mind.

After talking with Justin, she'd gone upstairs when Kyle whimpered in his sleep. He'd been up every couple of hours during the night with a stuffy nose until finally she'd sat in the chair with him in her arms. He was fitful but did get some sleep, and rest was the best thing for a cold. It was morning now, but she was still in the glider chair, moving back and forth with the baby in her arms.

She kissed his forehead, partly to assess his body temperature, but mostly because she needed him to know she cared. "I don't like it when you're not feeling well, sweetheart."

Justin walked into the nursery as he did every morning, freshly showered and shaved. He looked like a Hollywood heartthrob, while she resembled a back-to-nature reality show contestant who'd been on the island too long. She shouldn't care; it wasn't part of her job to be camera ready. Since she couldn't quite control the feeling, she acknowledged the flaw and let it go for now.

"Hi." She kept her voice soft and low.

His forehead creased with worry. "What's wrong?"

There was no point in asking how he knew that. The humidifier was going and this wasn't how the morning usually started.

"I had a bad feeling when I put Kyle to bed last night." Then she'd gone back downstairs and Justin had convinced her to attend the Crawfords' party. Her issues seemed so small when this little guy was sick.

"Why? What was up last night?"

"He was a little sniffly. More tired and cranky than usual." She lifted her shoulders in a shrug. It was hard to put that instinctive sensation into words. She *knew* this child so well and cared so deeply about him, she was tuned in to his needs. "Just a feeling. I didn't want to be right, but he has a cold."

"Did he sleep through the night?" Justin asked.

She shook her head. "About every hour he woke up crying. Finally, about four I just held him."

"Oh, Emma—" He dragged his fingers through his hair. "I didn't hear a thing. You should have gotten me up."

"I would have if there was something you could have done. But there was no point in both of us being tired. And you have to work today."

"Does he have a fever?"

"It's about a hundred. I've been giving him fluids and checking his diaper. It's wet, so he's well hydrated."

Justin started pacing. "I think Adam should take a look at him."

"I'm pretty sure it's just a virus." She looked at the baby when he whimpered in his sleep. "Unless something changes and his temperature spikes, it might be better to treat him at home rather than expose him to more germs at the clinic."

"I have connections there." He stopped in front of her and looked down, concern darkening his eyes. "He won't have to sit in the waiting room."

Emma nodded. "If that's what you want, I'll bring him in today."

"I'll call Adam. Kyle will be the first patient in and out before normal working hours start."

"Okay."

Justin used his cell to call the family practice doctor, who agreed to meet them before the clinic opened its doors. When he put the phone back on the case at his belt, she stood up and handed him the baby.

"I'll throw some clothes on."

Emma went to her room and dressed in jeans, sweater and boots. She ran a brush through her hair and sighed at the dark circles under her eyes.

"You should see the other guy," she said to her reflection.

Less than five minutes later she joined Justin in the nursery where Kyle was awake and fussy. She put fresh supplies in the diaper bag and looked at the sippy cup on the table beside the glider chair.

"I'll refill that and get him ready to go."

Justin stood and gave her the baby. "Let me do the cup."

"Okay. Half water, half ginger ale." She saw his disapproving look and said, "Now isn't the time to worry about nutrition. He likes it and will drink. The most important thing is making sure he's hydrated."

"You're not a pediatrician."

"Neither are you."

"But I am a doctor." Annoyance chased away the worry in his eyes for just a moment.

"But your specialty isn't babies. I've cared for a lot of little ones. They're not just small adults."

"I know that."

She blew out a long breath. "Look, we can stand here and argue about what he should drink or get him to someone you trust to tell us."

He nodded curtly. "I'll meet you downstairs."

"I can drive him to the clinic. Then you'll have your car there and won't have to bring us home."

"I'll drive." He walked out of the room before she could say anything else and that was just as well.

She put the fussy baby on the changing table and he rubbed his nose and eyes. The frustrated whimpering broke her heart.

"I know, sweetheart. I wish I could make you all better, but it just takes time."

She felt guilty for snapping at Justin. In spite of the one mistake that had landed the two of them in his bed, she and her boss got along really well. He was easygoing and a devoted father. Today he was a worried one and the tension made him short-tempered. She'd been up most of the night and was tired, which made for a volatile mix.

About twenty minutes later she and Justin were in exam room one at the clinic and Adam Stone was taking a look at the boy. Emma had met him at Kyle's one-year checkup and liked him very much. He was tall, dark and handsome, but on him it wasn't a cliché. Married to Blackwater Lake girl Jill Beck, he was a stepfather to her son, and the two had a baby of their own on the way. More important, he was a nice man and easy to talk to.

"His temp is just under a hundred," Adam said.

Justin was standing by the examination table trying to comfort his son, who was wearing nothing but a diaper. "He might need an antibiotic."

The other doctor said nothing as he cupped the rounded end of the stethoscope in his hands then placed it on Kyle's chest and back, listening intently. "Sounds good. You said he's not coughing?"

"That's right." Emma was standing beside her boss, aching to hold the baby but reluctant to overstep. Trying to figure out where she fit in here.

"I'll just have a look at his throat and ears."

Kyle wasn't the least bit happy at being manhandled this way and reached out to Emma, refusing to hold still. That did it. She didn't care if she was overstepping. No way would she stand by and watch when this baby was so upset and wanted her. She reached past Justin to pull the boy into her arms and he clung to her. In moments the hiccuping sobs started to subside.

"I'm sorry, Dr. Stone. But when he cries like that it breaks my heart. Would it be all right if I hold him while you do the examination?"

"Absolutely," he approved. "If he's calmer, I can get a better look at what's going on."

She cuddled the baby close and cooed to him reassuringly while the doctor listened to his back, then used a scope to check his ears. Kyle squirmed, but quieted when she whispered that everything was all right and just hold still a little longer. Dr. Stone actually managed to get a quick look in his throat, too.

"His nose is running from crying," he observed. "Any color to the secretions?"

"I don't think so." Justin looked blank for a moment then deferred to her. "Is there?"

"No. They've been clear." She rubbed her hand soothingly up and down Kyle's bare back as she swayed from side to side. "Is it okay if I get him dressed?"

"Sure." Adam had a wry expression on his face as he looked at his colleague. "You've got it bad, bud."

"What?"

"It's a syndrome a lot of doctors come down with when their kids get sick. The main symptom is forgetting everything you learned in med school."

Justin rubbed his neck. "So I'm overreacting?"

"Yeah. When the child is yours, you run on pure emotion. Logic and training go out the window. In a couple months when Jill has the baby, you can give me a hard time when my turn comes."

"I'm holding you to that," Justin promised. "So, Kyle is all right?"

"It looks like a virus and you know as well as I do that it just has to run its course. Antibiotics won't do anything unless he has a bacterial infection and prescribing them now runs the risk of him becoming resistant to them if he really needs one. Don't worry. He's going to be fine."

"That's what Emma said."

She was sliding denim overalls on Kyle but looked over her shoulder and smiled. "I didn't expect public acknowledgment."

Justin looked sheepish. "She told me it wasn't serious and hydration was the most important thing."

"She's right. Whatever you can get him to take. Clear liquids, even Popsicles."

"Ginger ale?" she asked sweetly.

"That's good." Adam nodded thoughtfully. "You probably already know this, but a slight fever isn't dangerous. It's the body's defenses kicking in to fight whatever is attacking. Keep an eye on it and use over-the-counter children's medication if necessary. If you're concerned about anything, call me."

"Thanks, Adam." Justin looked at her. "Consider this more public acknowledgment of your expertise. You were right about the ginger ale."

"He's a sturdy kid and has an excellent nanny," the other doctor said.

After he was dressed, Emma picked Kyle up from the exam table. "Thank you, Doctor."

"Anytime." He looked at Justin. "I'd like to talk to you about a patient. Do you have a minute?"

"Sure." He looked at her. "Would you mind waiting for me in the break room? You were also right about keeping him away from sick people."

"Not a problem," she told him.

Adam just grinned as she walked out and closed the door. She knew the room he wanted her to wait in was down the hall by the backdoor and walked there with the baby in her arms. A woman wearing pink scrubs was pouring herself a cup of coffee. Emma remembered nurse Ginny Irwin from Kyle's one-year checkup.

Her salt-and-pepper-colored hair was cut in a pixie style. Blue eyes snapped with intelligence and something that looked a lot like curiosity. "Hi, Emma."

"It's nice to see you again, Ginny." She smiled at the little boy, who shyly buried his face in her neck. "And you probably remember Kyle Flint."

"I do." She smiled, then stared at Emma as if she was trying to remember something. "You remind me of some-one."

She'd heard that before; people said it all the time. But, right here, right now, it meant something different. She knew her father and mother had been in the clinic yesterday. And before that, Maggie Potter had commented about her resemblance to Michelle.

"You know what they say—" She struggled to be casual. "Everyone has a double."

"Maybe." Ginny blew on her steaming coffee. "But I'd swear I've seen your double recently."

"Maybe I just have one of those faces." Her heart pounded and she hoped it didn't show. Explaining wouldn't be easy.

"Could be." She smiled at Kyle. "And speaking of that, he sure looks like his dad. This little boy is a cutie."

"That he is." As was his father.

"Nice to see you again. I'd love to stay and chat, but I need to get back to work."

"Don't let us hold you up. Have a good day." Emma returned the smile as the other woman left the room.

When she was alone, she let out a long breath. If Ginny recognized that she had a look-alike when they weren't even standing together, the resemblance to her mother must really be strong.

She'd looked nothing like the people who raised her and had never questioned it. What if there'd been a medical emergency and the truth came out with no warning? The shock would have been horrible. Since coming to Blackwater Lake she'd made her decisions based on her wish to spare the family any upset. But what if more people noticed the resemblance when they were together? And they would be together at the party.

She had to say something; she knew that. Now she wondered whether it would be easier to hear the news before or after the birthday party.

"Thanksgiving isn't for a couple of weeks. I could have gone grocery shopping for everything on my own," Emma said for the tenth time. "You didn't have to give up a day off to help."

Justin would have known she was in the car even if he couldn't see or hear her. The fragrance of flowers drifted around him and he was pretty sure that even Kyle, who was safely strapped in the backseat, could smell it. The three of them were just leaving the store parking lot and Justin checked traffic on his left before turning onto Main Street.

"Helping you buy and carry all that stuff is the least I could do to make up for being a jerk when Kyle was sick."

"Thank goodness he's better now."

"So you *were* worried." Justin made the turn, then glanced at her.

"Of course. But my concern was handled in a sensible, I've-got-a-plan way."

He appreciated her leaving out the part where his concern had manifested in an almost complete breakdown-of-rational-thought way. Glancing in the rearview mirror, he smiled at the bright-eyed little boy looking out the window and chattering away in the backseat. Halloween had come and gone. It had been a week since Kyle had been sick, but Justin still felt bad for taking out his anxiety on Emma. What was that saying? *You always hurt the ones you love*....

No, it wasn't that. He couldn't think of a label for this *thing* simmering between them, but no way he'd call it love.

"Next time he's under the weather, I promise to defer to your wisdom," he vowed.

"I'll believe that when I see it." Her tone was brimming with amusement.

"How can you say that?" he protested. "I'm guilty before the fact?"

"We hope Kyle will never be sick again, but that's probably not realistic. As you well know, Doctor, he has to take his immune system out for a spin every now and then to exercise it. And when that happens, there's every reason to believe you'll do the same thing."

"Which was?"

"You'll behave like any other loving father would."

"But I'm a trained physician. I know better."

"There's no way to be objective when your child is the patient. Under those circumstances, a little knowledge is a dangerous thing. Knowing the worst makes it harder to stay calm."

He heard the patient understanding in her voice that somehow was approval of how he'd acted. The words were like a pardon and made him feel closer to her somehow. Like they were partners. Like... Nope, couldn't go there either.

Keep it light. "So, helping with the shopping is my penance for going into freak-out mode."

"Apparently you're a steadfast believer in do the crime, do the time?"

"It's fair to say that, yes."

"I'm not sure about this. Lugging an eighteen-pound lump of frozen poultry, plus all the rest of the Thanksgiving dinner fixings, seems like an out-of-proportion penance for behavior that was completely human and understandable."

He glanced over and thought how ordinary and special it was to have her there. She was sweet, steady, sexy and stunning. If things were different, he could be thinking that he was the luckiest guy in the world that she was with him. They could be any teasing, laughing couple out with their son. But that wasn't the way it was. If he reminded himself enough, maybe he would stop wanting her so badly.

"Human," he said. "You're very diplomatic, Miss Robbins. Sylvia would have had some colorful things to say about my behavior."

"If that's a challenge, you should know that I can be colorful," she defended.

"Okay. Right here, right now, dispensation from professional. Go for it. Be colorful."

"Let's see." She tapped her lip. "All right. Here goes.

You were a little insufferable, maybe a tad condescending. Just a bit egotistical and dismissive."

"Really? That's all you've got?" He laughed. "Sounded more classy than colorful."

"I've got more, but…" She angled her head toward the baby in the backseat. "Little ears. Kids absorb a lot more than adults realize. And Kyle is starting to repeat the sounds he hears."

"Then thank goodness he hears you. What he learns will be refined. Not to mention the extensive vocabulary he'll pick up."

"Please tell me that's not you putting pressure on him. You're not going to be one of those demanding fathers who makes his son study every waking moment. You know the kind. The one who goes ballistic over a B+ in school because it's not an A."

He heard the teasing in her voice and quickly looked over at her. "Have you met me? Do you not see what a marshmallow I am with him?"

There was laughter in her eyes. "So, you're one of those permissive parents whose child can do no wrong?"

He braked at a stoplight and rested his forearm on the steering wheel, thinking that over. "I could probably get behind that philosophy."

"I see we need to have an in-service on the merits of balance in parenting."

"Are you mocking me? Is that sass?"

"Probably. But only because you gave me a dispensation from being professional."

"Remind me not to do that again, Emma."

From the backseat Kyle said, "Mama—"

She half turned and looked at him. "Hey, sweet pea. Did you say Em-ma?"

"Mama," he said again, distinctly pronouncing both syllables.

"He's trying to say Emma. You know that, right?"

"I know."

And yet, mothering came so naturally to her that it seemed right somehow to call her that. Anyone could see how much she loved this child. In a perfect world, she would be Kyle's mother, but the world was far from perfect. There were no legal ties binding her to them. She worked for him and could move on anytime. The thought of that bothered him so much more now than it had during her interview.

He met her gaze for a moment, then the light turned green and he drove on. "Would it bother you if that name stuck?"

"Would it bother you?" she countered.

"It's as close to giving him balance as possible," he finally said. "He doesn't have a mother and will never know what it would have been like to have her in his life."

"And that bothers you. Even though you mentioned her—flaws."

He nodded and turned the car right, driving around the lake. "He'll never have a two-parent home, something most kids take for granted."

"I think what you need to focus on is what he *does* have."

"And what's that?" he asked.

"You." Her full lips curved into a smile. "There are a lot of children who don't have mothers or fathers. They're being raised by grandparents or other relatives. Or in the foster-care system. Or on their own, not knowing where the next meal is coming from. Kyle has a father who loves him enough to be an insufferable jerk when he's worried, but his mother is gone. Will that make him different in school?" She shrugged. "Maybe. But it's his reality and he'll adjust to what is."

"So you don't think he'll turn to drugs and alcohol to fill the void?" he joked.

"Did I mention that you have a flair for the dramatic?" She laughed. "He'll learn his values from his environment and unless there's something I don't know about, his surroundings are pretty okay."

"You think he'll be all right?" That was a completely serious question, because it would always be a concern.

"He'll make friends who are drawn to the bright, funny boy he is. People will like him or not for himself. Not who you are or because his mother isn't around."

He turned into his driveway and pressed the automatic door opener, then drove into the garage. "Are you saying I should let it go?"

"Yes."

That was good advice and he'd take it. He opened his car door. "Okay, then. Let's take this stuff inside."

"I'll get Kyle. You take the groceries."

"How is that balance?" He met her gaze before she got out of the SUV.

"You're still doing penance." She grinned, then slid to the ground.

That wicked smile cracked open a nugget of need that most of the time he managed to shut down, but right now he couldn't do it. Fortunately, she was busy getting the baby out of the car seat and didn't notice the longing Justin knew was in his eyes.

"I'm going to give him lunch, then put him down for a nap."

He reached into the rear of the SUV and grabbed several grocery bags at once. "He doesn't look tired to me."

"Trust me," she said. "He is."

Just then the little boy rubbed his eyes and yawned. Justin supposed that's what they called a "mom thing." A woman didn't have to give birth to know a child. His wife had carried Kyle inside her and had never bothered to get to know him. She'd been more concerned about her post-baby body.

As he carried everything into the house, Emma put Kyle in the high chair and gave him finger food while she assembled his lunch. He got some of it in, but then turned crabby and threw his sippy cup on the floor.

"He's done." She lifted him out of the chair and hugged him close. "I'll take him upstairs and clean him up. Then little man is going down for a nap."

Justin nodded and put the turkey in the freezer. After starting to unpack the grocery bags, it instantly became clear that he didn't have a clue where anything went. In surgery he had a system and wanted scalpel, gauze and sutures placed exactly the same way every time. He wanted to be able to find them with his eyes closed. Obviously the kitchen wasn't an operating room, but Emma would want to be able to find things.

It wasn't long before she was back with the baby monitor. "He's out cold."

"Already?"

"It's that time of the day." She looked at the boxes and cans littering the kitchen island and started putting them away. Holding the boxed stuffing in her hand, a sad look slipped into her eyes. "It just occurred to me."

"What?"

"This is the first Thanksgiving without my mother."

She'd had the same feelings around Halloween and Justin knew she was still grieving. Every holiday without the woman she'd thought was her mother would be difficult. There was a reason that the mourning period in the olden days officially lasted a year. But the woman had stolen Emma's life.

"She wasn't your mother. The woman kidnapped you." He knew it was probably the wrong thing to say but couldn't stop the words.

"I know." There was confusion and frustration in those two words. "What she did was wrong. But she never gave me reason to question whether or not she was my mother. She loved me, raised me."

"I can see how much you care for Kyle. Like a mother. Like you were cared for, but she robbed your real mother of that." Justin hated seeing her so tortured, but he had to say this. "Your mother would want to know that you're alive, and well, and happy."

"What are you saying?"

"I would never tell you what to do," he said. "But put yourself in her place. What if someone took Kyle? How would you feel? Wouldn't you want to know that he was all right? I certainly would."

She stared at him for several moments, then turned away and covered her face with her hands. Her shoulders shook with sobs.

"Emma— Damn it."

Justin moved close and put his hands on her arms, then turned her against his chest. He wrapped his arms around her and pressed a kiss to her hair. "I'm sorry. That was uncalled for. I shouldn't have pushed. Please don't cry. You can add lout, oaf and boor to that list of colorful adjectives."

She let out a sound that was part sob, part laugh. "It's okay. You're right about this." She looked up at him, tears streaking her face. "I've already made up my mind to tell them who I am, but after the party. I don't want to do anything to spoil Michelle's day."

"That's good." He studied her face.

Her cheeks were blotchy and there was distress in her eyes. But he saw something else, too. Yearning. Desire. Longing—everything he was feeling. And suddenly the need to comfort wasn't nearly as strong as the need to kiss her. The wanting was so big it pushed out shouldn't, wouldn't, couldn't.

He could and did.

He kissed her.

Chapter Eleven

Emma sighed at the touch of Justin's lips. Her mind had barely absorbed the sudden shift in mood, when he was kissing the tears from her cheeks and her heart went all mushy. In truth, it wasn't completely unexpected. Promises to be scrupulously professional had not smothered the sparks flaring between them. Right this minute she couldn't remember and didn't care about anything but being as close to this man as possible.

She slid her arms around his waist and he deepened the kiss, then traced her lips until she opened to him. He stroked the roof of her mouth and fire exploded through her. In a heartbeat the sound of their labored breathing filled the kitchen.

Just as suddenly, he took a step back and pulled her arms away, then brought one of her palms to his lips and pressed a kiss there. "I'm sorry."

She blinked at him. "For kissing me?"

"I'll never regret that." Tenderly he grazed her cheek with his knuckles. "I didn't mean to make you cry. I'd never hurt you. It's just that the words were out before

I thought them through. It's none of my business. I'm sorry—"

She touched a finger to his lips to stop him. "It's all right."

His jaw and his eyes turned the color of clouds growing into a thunderstorm. "That's not all."

"What's wrong?" she asked.

"Emma—" He blew out a long breath. "I don't want to want you."

"I know." She couldn't look at him now because she knew what she had to do. "Everything will be much simpler if I just go upstairs."

"It would be simpler." He squeezed her hands and didn't let go. "But in my opinion, simple is highly overrated."

The meaning of his words sank in and her gaze jumped to his, where need burned in his eyes. "Give me complicated any day of the week."

"I was hoping you'd say that." Then he looked at the baby monitor on the counter. "Kyle—"

"He usually naps for an hour or so."

"Or so..."

Justin threaded his fingers through hers and they walked to his room. Bright sunshine shone through the window as if smiling on them. They stood by the bed, close enough to feel the body heat but not touching.

He leaned down and when his lips touched hers, every single cell in her body responded. Being here with Justin felt too darn good to regret anything. Suddenly heat accumulated beneath her clothes and she yanked them off as fast as possible. Justin did the same and she shamelessly looked at the lean, hard lines of his body.

To look and not touch was like dieting in a bakery. She rested her hand on his chest and savored the arousing texture of the coarse dusting of hair that tickled her palm.

Dragging a fingertip over the contour of muscle, she marveled at the beauty of his male form.

As her fingers trailed over his stomach, Justin sucked in a breath and caught her hand. Rays of sunshine coming through the window made the tension in his eyes glitter as he drew her onto the bed. After sliding under the covers, he kissed her, a slow insatiable kiss that was edgy and exciting. He dragged his mouth over her cheek and jaw then took her earlobe between his teeth and gently tugged until tingles danced over her shoulders and down her breasts.

Shivering with need, she turned on her side to face him and met his hungry lips with her own, wanting more of the whole-mouthed kisses that rocked her soul. At the same time, his hand cupped her breast, tracing lazy erotic circles over the sensitive softness until her skin burned and heat gathered everywhere. He slid lower, cupping her as one finger entered her.

"I can't wait, Justin," she gasped. "I need you now."

"Yes—" His voice was ragged, his breathing labored.

He left her long enough to open the nightstand drawer and then she heard the effective rip of the foil packet he'd grabbed. When he'd covered himself, he rolled to her again and took her in his arms.

With a grin, he pulled her on top. "I want to see all the expressions on your face."

It was her nature to be shy, but she wasn't with Justin. She straddled his hips and lowered herself slowly until they were one. Pleasure roared through her as sensations rushed fierce and fast. Too soon shudders began spilling over her in waves that made her light-headed with pleasure. He gathered her to his chest and held her until it was over. Gently, he rolled her to her back and settled on top, then slowly moved inside her.

His face was taut with tension and concentration as

he rocked against her, his thrusts lengthening until he groaned. Emma wrapped her arms around him and kissed his shoulder until he was still and spent. They stayed locked together for a long time before he sighed and slid away, leaving the bed to go into the bathroom.

Though the last thing she wanted was to move, Emma forced herself to get up. She dressed quickly and went to the kitchen where some groceries still waited to be put away. Her mind was racing, mostly telling her one time in his bed was a fluke. Twice was a pattern.

Before she was ready to face him, Justin walked into the room fully dressed, carefully staying just inside the doorway to keep his distance.

"Emma, I—"

"Don't." She met his gaze and panic skipped over her raw nerves. "Please. Let's not talk about it."

He slid his fingers into his jeans pockets. "We're going to have to at some point."

She wanted to tell him if they both worked really hard, it would be possible to ignore what just happened. But that wouldn't make the problem disappear any more than doing nothing had resolved her family issues. She was through running away from it.

"You're right."

"It was a moment of weakness," he said.

That was an understatement. "What are we going to do about that?"

"Not be alone together."

There was a tone in his voice saying what she had already realized: How were they going to pull that off what with living in the same house? She knew the answer but couldn't bring herself to say it.

And then Emma heard a sleepy, waking-up sound come through the baby monitor. "This discussion needs to wait for a bit. I have a lot of thinking to do and when we talk, there probably shouldn't be distractions."

More echoey, little-boy chatter squawked from the nursery and Justin nodded. "I agree. Do you want me to get him?"

"That's okay." She felt the need to hold the baby while she could. "I'll go."

She hurried up the stairs and her thoughts seemed to move just as fast. Earlier, Justin had said that he shouldn't have brought up anything about telling her family the truth, that it was none of his business. But he was wrong. The fallout from her revelation would affect everything and she was tired of wondering what it would be.

She was ready to resolve her life. It was the reason that she'd stayed in Blackwater Lake, and the time had come to do it. She could easily fall in love with her boss and she needed to tell her family who she was and give Justin notice that she was leaving town before she couldn't leave him at all. He'd made it clear that he wasn't interested in anything serious. If she stayed, she'd never be more than the hired help and an occasional lover.

That would destroy her.

Emma had never been so fidgety and nervous in her life. She and Justin had just pulled to a stop at the curb just up the street from the Crawford house, where her parents were inside. A lot of other cars were parked up and down the street, so they weren't the first ones to arrive.

Justin turned off the ignition and opened his door, letting the car's overhead light turn on. "Are you ready?"

"Yes."

"That's a lie."

"Busted." When had he come to know her so well?

"But I'll never be ready for this, so at least I can be punctual for the party."

"That's the spirit."

"Do you think Kyle is all right with Maggie?" They had just dropped the little guy off at the Potters' house. She touched the handle but didn't pull it to open the car door.

"I'm sure he's fine. He has excellent taste in friends, by the way. Danielle is very cute."

"She takes after her mom."

At play group that week Emma had mentioned the upcoming party and Maggie had offered to take Kyle for a couple of hours so the two little ones could play together. She wasn't going to the party but knew about it because her mother was a friend of the Crawfords and would be there along with town business owners, professionals and longtime friends. The staff from Mercy Medical Clinic were all planning to attend.

"Don't worry, Emma. Maggie has both of our cellphone numbers. If she needs us, she'll call."

"I know. You're right. It's just that this is the first time I've left him."

"Now you know how I feel every day." The interior light revealed his wry expression. "And you, Miss Robbins, are procrastinating."

"I was kind of hoping you hadn't noticed."

"Nothing gets by me." He grinned. "Mostly. Come on. Whatever happens, I'm right there with you."

"Thanks."

"Don't mention it."

When he slid out and shut the door, the SUV interior went dark, letting the night back in. She suddenly felt cold, alone and anxious. A single word of gratitude seemed totally inadequate when the truth was that she wouldn't have gotten this far without Justin Flint. It wasn't only the job that had made it possible for her to stay, but also the favor of a shoulder to lean on and someone to talk to. The dark was a reminder of how alone she was going to be when she had to quit her job.

But that wasn't happening tonight.

She opened the car door and slid to the ground. Justin was there and rested his hand at the small of her back as they moved down the street toward the house, then stepped up on the curb and walked along the curved sidewalk to the Crawfords' front door. The path was lined with vividly colored fall flowers and there was grass on either side. Her parents lived in a neat, two-story white clapboard house with hunter-green trim and a matching front door. There was a wraparound front porch with white Adirondack chairs where they could sit and greet neighbors who walked by or watch their children playing on the lawn.

Emma realized she had no idea how the woman she'd thought was her mother had managed to abduct her and get away with it. Suddenly she wanted to know how it all went down, and these people had the answer.

The sound of voices drifted to the porch from inside the house. Quite a few guests were already here. Justin rang the bell and a few moments later the door was opened by Alan Crawford.

He grinned. "Glad you could make it, Justin."

"Me, too. Thanks for the invitation. You know Emma."

"Hi." When did her throat get so dry?

"I've seen you in the diner. Nice to finally meet you."

"Same here," she managed to say.

He closed the door, then looked at Justin. "You should know that Michelle wasn't surprised. She figured out what I was up to a couple days ago. Still don't know how I tipped her off. Fair warning, Justin. She said men aren't subtle. Whatever that means."

"When you figure it out, let me know."

"Take a number," he said ruefully.

Emma smiled at the banter as she nervously looked around the inside of the house where her parents lived. One thing she'd learned in her time as a nanny is that a person's surroundings contained clues about their character. Michelle and Alan Crawford had a warm and spotless environment, if the entryway was anything to go by. The two-story entry had a dark wood floor and brass coat rack by the front door where jackets, hats and scarves were hanging. A chandelier hung from the high ceiling and was shining on the dark maple banister and railing, Framed pictures of lakes and mountains hung on the expanse of wall that joined the two floors and there was a wooden bench at the bottom.

"Hang your coats on the rack," Alan said. "Or you can put them on the bench there."

"How's the arm?" Justin asked, taking off his jacket and holding his hand out for hers.

The other man made a fist and flexed his forearm. He was wearing a sweater over his checked cotton shirt and the bandage was hidden. "It's healing nicely. No pain anymore."

"Glad to hear it." He hung up their coats.

"The birthday girl is in the living room," he said. "What can I get you to drink?"

"Beer for me," Justin said. He looked at her and his expression said he was wondering how she was doing.

"Do you have a chardonnay?" she asked.

"It's Michelle's favorite. Coming right up. I'm pretty sure you know a lot of people here. Go on in and make yourselves at home." Alan moved down a hall that presumably led to the kitchen.

"You okay?" Concern darkened Justin's eyes.

"As well as can be expected." She glanced at the place where the man disappeared. It would take a while to think of him as her father, if she ever could. "He seems nice."

"He is. Shall we go say happy birthday?"

There was no getting out of it now. Again he put his hand on her lower back. It was touches like this that contributed to her "moments of weakness." but right this minute she was very grateful to have him there.

His fingers were warm, his smile encouraging. Her heart skipped a beat and she was almost certain that would never change. She could and would have taken this step alone, but his steady presence helped her put one foot in front of the other. And when it was all over, she knew he would be there with a shoulder to cry on or as someone simply to talk to.

They turned left into a large room where the wood floor continued. An area rug contained a grouping of furniture that included two hunter-green floral-covered love seats and a couple of club chairs. The conversation area had a coffee table in the center. Ben McKnight and Camille Halliday sat on one love seat with Adam Stone and his wife, Jill, on the other. All of them waved a greeting.

Emma recognized Mayor Goodson, an attractive brunette who could be anywhere from thirty to fifty. She was leading Blackwater Lake's robust development, a strategy that included a summer and winter resort that would break ground soon.

"Who's that man standing by the love seat with the attractive brunette? The couple talking to Ben?" Emma looked up at Justin.

"Ben's brother, Alex, and his fiancée, Ellie Hart."

"Looks like they're having fun." And she wasn't just referring to the fact that all three women had varying sizes of baby bump. Love? Or something in Blackwater Lake's water? She wouldn't put her money on magic. If it existed, Justin might have been tempted to take another chance on love.

"That looks like a couples area." His tone said it was a place he didn't want to go. "And we're on a mission. Remember? Mingle with your family."

"Right." Knowing them a little better might make it easier to tell them who she was after the party was over. In a day or two.

As they walked farther into the room, people greeted Justin. It seemed practically everyone had been to Mercy Medical Clinic. More impressive, he remembered all the names and introduced her. Unfortunately, the detour just fed the tension growing inside her. Eventually they made it to where Michelle was standing with another woman beside the large fireplace, which had an impressive oak mantel. A roaring fire was going there. The two were obviously friends and as they moved closer, she extended her good wishes to the birthday girl and moved away.

Michelle smiled warmly. "I'm so glad you both could come."

"Me, too," Justin said. "I believe you've met Emma."

"Yes. How are you?"

"Good," she lied. "Happy birthday."

"Thank you."

Emma hesitated a moment, trying to think of something to say. Then she recalled what Alan had told them.

"How did you find out about the surprise party?"

Michelle's eyes twinkled. "When you've known someone as long as I've known Alan, it's pretty tough to get away with anything."

"How long have you known each other?" she asked.

"We were high school sweethearts."

"That's a while—" Emma realized what she'd said and

stopped. "I mean—" She shook her head. "There's no recovery from that. Let me just say you look fantastic."

"For my age." The woman grinned good-naturedly.

"For *any* age," Emma said sincerely.

It wasn't like looking in the mirror. More a preview of how she might weather the years. Awfully darn well if she'd inherited this woman's DNA. The lovely skin was relatively unlined and her trim shape showed that she took good care of herself.

"Life does march on and leaves footprints on a face," she said honestly. "There's a reason it's called a time line."

And life had thrown her a major curve, Emma thought. She'd been knocked around but hadn't gone down. That was impressive.

"So, you met your husband in high school. When did you two get married?"

"Right after graduation," she said.

"Your parents didn't have a problem with both of you being so young?" Emma asked.

"They just knew we were determined to be together and bowed to the pressure. And I'm glad to say they never regretted supporting our decision." She smiled, remembering. "I had the first of three boys about a year later." She glanced at the mantel beside her with lots of framed photographs sitting there.

Emma followed her gaze and realized the pictures were all family, individual and group. Dead center of all the frames was a photograph of an infant dressed all in pink.

It was a baby picture, a child roughly six weeks old. That had to be Emma and it was the only one. She couldn't seem to stop looking at it. Had she been stolen shortly after the photo was taken? Or like the average family who thinks they have all the time in the world, did they just get too busy to take more?

"That's Sarah Elizabeth."

Emma's gaze snapped back to the woman and there were tears in her eyes. From newspaper articles about the kidnapping she'd known the name she was given at birth. But hearing it from her mother's lips… What was she supposed to say?

"I'm sure you heard that she was kidnapped. It was a long time ago, but people remember. We'll always be the couple who own the diner and lost their little girl."

Profound pain brimmed in her mother's eyes and broke Emma's heart. "You don't have to talk about it. This is a happy occasion. It's your birthday."

"Mostly I don't say anything, but sometimes I find myself thinking about her and the words just come out." She wiped a tear from her cheek. "I'm sorry."

Emma touched her arm, a gesture of comfort. "It's all right."

"I didn't mean to do that." The other woman's mouth trembled when she tried to smile. "It's just that every once in a while I can't hold back the thoughts. Where is my child? How is she? Is she happy? Is she all right?"

This was the moment Emma had come to Blackwater Lake for and instantly her uncertainty disappeared. There was no question in her mind about the right thing to do. Her parents were in conflict every single day because of not knowing what happened to their child.

To *her.*

If Kyle disappeared, the not knowing would be hell. Justin was right. She looked up at him now and he nodded slightly, encouraging her. It was way past time to end her family's nightmare. Party or not, she had to tell them and knew now how wrong she'd been to wait so long.

She was about to say something when Alan walked

over with drinks in his hand. He gave the beer to Justin. "Here you go. And I have a glass of white wine for you."

A cold drink would feel good on her dry throat, maybe dislodge the lump there, but Emma's hand was trembling too badly to take it.

She shook her head, then looked at each of her parents. After taking a deep breath, she said, "You might want to sit down because I have something to tell you both."

Chapter Twelve

Emma hadn't let herself have any expectations about her family, let alone prepare for this moment if it ever came. She usually didn't have trouble speaking her mind, but she was at a loss for words now. The sound of conversation around them disappeared as if some mysterious force had dropped a cone of silence.

Michelle's expression went from curious to just this side of anxious. "What is it, Emma?"

"Why do we have to sit down?" Alan asked.

Justin cleared his throat. "Is there somewhere we can go that's quiet? With no people around?"

"They're everywhere," Michelle answered. "Kitchen, family room, dining room. Even the backyard. I don't understand— Why do we have to go somewhere private? It's never a good thing when someone says that."

"No one's in the garage," her husband said.

"Let's go there," Justin quickly said before either of them could ask more questions. He put his hand on Emma's elbow, a small bit of contact that was both encouraging and reassuring. "Trust me, you're going to want privacy for this conversation."

"You know what this is about?" Michelle's expression was even more apprehensive when she looked at him. "Now you're starting to scare me. Please, just say it."

"Justin's right. Let's go in the garage," Emma said.

Again, not the setting she'd pictured, but there probably wasn't a chapter in any etiquette book to cover this situation. She looked at her father. "Lead the way."

He nodded grimly and offered the white wine he was still holding to his wife. When she shook her head, he set the glass on an end table then took her hand and led her through the house. They filed past the family room, where guests milled around, and finally turned down a hall. They walked through a door in the laundry room and into the cold, dark garage.

Alan flipped a switch on the wall and a dim bulb overhead flashed on. As garages went, it was average except for one thing. There was a place for everything and everything in its place. Overhead suspension storage held bins of what looked like Christmas decorations. Tall white cabinets lined the walls and there was a workbench with Peg-Board above it for tools. Two vehicles were parked side by side, one a truck, the other a compact car.

"There's nowhere to sit unless we pull out the folding chairs." Alan put his arm around his wife's shoulders. "So, whatever it is, just say it. We've had more than our share of bad and we're still standing."

Emma could see him bracing for something awful. "Well, I hope this isn't bad. I don't think it is after what you said about wanting to know where your daughter is."

"You know something about our little girl?" Michelle's voice broke.

Emma met her gaze and saw fear and hope in the other woman's eyes. No more dragging this out. It must be excruciating for them. "I *am* your daughter."

There was complete silence for several moments as they stared at her. Probably she should have taken her father up on the offer to get out folding chairs.

Emma felt compelled to fill the hushed quiet. "I found out because my—" She couldn't call the woman "mother." That woman had turned their lives upside down and let Emma grow up living a lie. She was looking at her mother, the one who'd brought her into this world, and saw tragedy and pain on her face. With all her heart she wanted to erase it.

"The woman who took me only confessed the truth when she was dying. She gave me your names and told me where to find you."

Then she stopped, letting them absorb the information and steeled herself for skepticism and anger. They'd probably want a DNA test.

"You look just like your mother did in high school." Alan's voice was soft and cracked with emotion. "I can't believe I didn't see it."

"You weren't looking," Justin said.

"Maggie Potter saw." Michelle reached up and clutched the hand her husband had put on her shoulder. "At lunch that day when she had Danielle and you brought Kyle in with you. She noticed our eyes were the same color and the shape of our faces is similar. But I never thought—"

"I remember."

The other woman stared at her as if she couldn't look hard enough. As if she might disappear. "Does Maggie know who you really are?"

"No."

"But Justin obviously does," the woman continued.

"I felt it was necessary to tell him. Whatever happened would affect him and his son. I hate lies and should have been completely honest at the initial interview, but I wasn't sure what to do if I didn't get the job." Instead of firing her, he'd been nothing but caring and sympathetic in letting her find her way.

"Let me get this straight." Michelle blinked as if everything was slowly sinking in. "You've been here in Blackwater Lake all this time? Right here in town and didn't tell us that you're alive and well?"

"Yes. I'm sorry." And she felt incredible guilt. "I just knew everything would change. It was such a shock to me, finding out. I can't explain—"

"You've grown into such a beautiful young woman."

Her mother didn't sound angry, but Emma wondered how she couldn't be. "I didn't want to cause you more pain, or upset you. It sounds so silly now, but—"

Michelle's eyes filled with tears, this time joyful ones. She smiled. "I'm the complete opposite of upset. There are no words to express what I'm feeling. This is a moment I'd given up hope of ever having. I think that's why it didn't sink in when Maggie pointed out the strong resemblance. After so many years without a word, you just give up. Come here, baby." She pulled Emma into her arms. "My daughter. My girl."

Emma had so many feelings rolling through her, but mostly she felt a sense of peace and rightness. And emotion. Tears filled her eyes as she held the other woman and they stayed like that for a long time. Finally she pulled back.

Her mother put a shaking hand on her cheek and with her thumb brushed the wetness away. "Can you believe this, Alan? She didn't want to upset us."

Her father shook his head and his eyes were moist when he gently tugged her into a quick, hard hug. "No, I can't believe this. We thought about you every single day and prayed. Both of us thought it but we couldn't say out loud that we believed you were never coming back. I never knew being wrong could feel so good."

When he let her go, Emma looked at them. "I'll take a DNA test." She met Justin's gaze and he nodded slightly, letting her know he'd make it happen. "Then there will be no doubt."

"All right. But I'm absolutely sure you're my child," her mom said. "The family resemblance is unmistakable. You'll see when you meet your brothers. They're here, you know."

"That's going to be weird," she said. "But I've always wanted a big brother."

"How about three?" Alan grinned.

"The more the merrier," she said.

"DNA." Michelle shook her head as if to say that was a foolish idea. "If looks aren't enough proof for you, the innate kindness you showed in not wanting to upset us is a giveaway. It's something your father would do."

"Not you?" Emma asked.

She shook her head. "I upset people on a fairly regular basis."

"Your mother is fibbing, big-time."

"Then there's her choice of career," the big fibber went on. "Only someone who loves children would work with them like you do."

"That's just like your mom," Alan explained. "She couldn't wait to have babies."

Emma didn't think this was the time to tell them that the woman who took her also loved children, but her way of showing it was self-centered and destructive. This wasn't the time for that conversation.

Instead, she said, "I always knew I wanted to work with children—" She glanced at Justin, quietly supportive through this whole surreal nightmare and silently heroic right now. He was just watching over all of them. "In so many ways Justin made this reunion possible. If not for him I might not be here now. He gave me a job so I could earn a living while I was conflicted about what to do. He never pushed, but the way he loves his son finally convinced me that telling you was the only thing to do."

Alan held out his hand. "Thanks, Doc. For taking care of our girl. We're grateful to you for that."

"My pleasure." He smiled at her and even in such dim light the heat in his eyes was evident.

Emma felt the effects of that look all the way to her toes and the reaction showed no sign of weakening any time soon. There were decisions to make but this wasn't the time or place to make them.

"Justin—" Michelle stopped and just gave him a big hug. "I don't have the words. But nothing says thank-you like free meals at the diner for life."

"It's not necessary but much appreciated," he said. "And I'm not noble. Emma is really something. She's terrific with Kyle and a great cook. My guess is that she takes after one or both of you in that department."

Words of praise had never bothered Emma before. Really, who didn't want to hear they were doing a good job? But that was the point. He was talking about her work performance, when the reason she put her heart and soul into everything she did for him was profoundly personal.

She cared very deeply about Justin Flint and his son. None of it felt like a job.

Her father sighed. "I can see why you wanted to tell us about this quietly, Justin. Thank you for that, too. And breaking up this reunion is the last thing I want." He cocked his thumb toward the door leading into the house. "But there's a birthday party going on and folks are going to notice that the guest of honor is missing."

"Right." Her mother looked uncertain. "My daughter coming home is the best gift I've ever had. It's going to be practically impossible to keep it to myself. Your brothers will want to meet you. Do you mind if we share the news now?"

"I'm okay with whatever you want," Emma said. "You're the birthday girl."

"All right, then. It's efficient to let half the town know now so that when the rumor spreads maybe it will be something close to the truth." She linked her arm with Emma's. "Let's go announce the best possible news, sweetie."

The endearment warmed Emma's heart more than she'd thought possible. It wasn't comfortable with them yet, but she had a mother, father and three brothers. A family who was happy to have her home. She wasn't alone any longer.

She glanced at Justin and felt her heart drop as a realization hit hard. Her past was finally settled; her future was anything but.

Justin pulled into the driveway and stopped the SUV next to the empty space where Emma's car was usually parked. But tonight it wasn't there. He'd had a surgery that went late and told her this morning not to expect him for dinner. In the afternoon he'd received a text from her letting him know she and Kyle might be at her parents' when he got home. They'd been invited for dinner.

She'd seen them every day since telling them her true identity over a week ago. And he was glad she was getting to know the family.

He got out of the car and walked up the steps. The windows were dark and that was different, not in a good way. The house hadn't been dark when he arrived home from the clinic ever. First, Sylvia had been there with Kyle, and now Emma. But not tonight. After unlocking and opening the door, he flipped on the light switch in the entryway. At least he could see his way now, even if the strangeness didn't go away. His first stop was the office, where he left the paperwork he'd brought home.

Then he went to the kitchen. Like the rest of the place, this room was unwelcoming. There were no good smells or happy baby sounds. Even unhappy ones. Especially there was no cheerful female chatter. No laughter. It was as if the house was missing its heart.

"And that weird, whimsical thought deserves a beer," he said to himself.

He opened the refrigerator and grabbed a longneck from the shelf on the door. In front of him was a plate of pasta covered with plastic wrap and beside it sat a salad. On the wrap was a note.

Justin: In case I'm not back when you get home there's balsamic vinaigrette dressing, your fave, for the salad. Put the plate in the microwave and hit the button that says—wait for it—plate. =) Emma.

For the first time since turning into the driveway, he smiled. Each word written in her familiar, neat, artistic handwriting was wrapped in her voice. It made him miss her more.

After tossing the salad and warming the food, everything was on the table beside his half-empty beer bottle. A place setting for one. The high chair was neatly tucked away by the wall and there wasn't another plate out. Everything just felt wrong.

And then he heard the front door open. A few moments later Emma appeared in the kitchen doorway with Kyle in her arms. He was sound asleep with his head on her shoulder, so obviously she'd managed to get him out of the car seat without waking him.

She moved closer and whispered, "He went out like a light on the drive. I know you like to spend time with him in the evening and I can wake him—"

"No. He looks so peaceful." At least one of the Flint men was.

"Worn-out is more like it." For a quick moment she touched her cheek to the baby's, an automatic tender gesture that clearly showed how deep her feelings went. "I'm going to put him to bed."

"Okay."

The sight of her and Kyle lifted Justin's mood some. The house was just as quiet, but knowing she was there smoothed over a restlessness he'd never known before. Day in and day out he'd been so consumed with seeing her, wanting her and not having her that there was no room to wonder what it would feel like without her.

Now he had a clue.

It wasn't long before she was back. Justin knew he was going to hell, but couldn't stop the rush of thank-you-God that the baby was settled and they were alone.

She looked at the table. "I can see you found dinner. Do you want me to heat it up?"

"Already done. It's a big portion. We can share it."

"I couldn't eat another bite. Michelle and Alan fixed a great dinner."

Justin nodded. "Why don't you keep me company while I eat?"

She glanced around the kitchen, either looking for an excuse to avoid him or just making sure nothing needed her attention. Then she smiled.

"Okay."

They sat across from each other and he took a long drink from his bottle of beer. "So, how was your day?"

"Really good." The happy smile made her radiant and more beautiful than ever. "How was yours? The procedure went well?"

"Perfect. It's delicate work, transplanting skin to cover a wound that doesn't want to heal. But I think there will be a positive outcome now."

"I'm glad."

As always, she didn't ask who the patient was. She already knew that privacy concerns prevented him from saying anything and didn't push. There were rules, even in a town as small as Blackwater Lake.

"Pasta is really good," he said after taking a bite.

"I got the recipe from Michelle. She's an amazing cook. I can learn a lot from her."

"You're a pretty incredible cook yourself."

"Thank you." But she shook her head, an awed expression on her face. "But I'm nothing like her."

"So it sounds as if you're getting to know them."

"Yes." She folded her arms on the table. "I can't believe how silly it was not to tell them the truth right away."

If that had happened, Justin thought, she never would have applied for the nanny job and he wouldn't have gotten to know her. Now it was hard to remember a time when she hadn't been here, in his life.

"I'm glad it's going well." Justin chewed a bite of salad and couldn't miss her serene expression.

"They're wonderful people. We've been bonding over the smallest things. Like how we talk with our hands. Certain gestures. Facial expressions."

He finished off the salad in the bowl, then said, "Inherited traits."

"Exactly. It's amazing when you think about it. Things

I have in common with Michelle and Alan. My brothers. Even though we didn't grow up together."

That surprised him. "Are they still here?"

"Yes. Even though the three of them have high-powered jobs and careers and aren't local." She shrugged. "I thought they'd leave right after the party, but they decided to juggle appointments and work remotely. To get to know me." She grinned. "I can't believe it. One day I'm all alone and the next I have a father, mother and three brothers. A real family."

What was he? Chopped liver. All this time with him had she felt abandoned? He'd done everything possible to make her feel included. Hadn't he?

Justin was happy things were working out for her, but a nagging feeling of discontent settled over him. After eating half the pasta, he pushed the plate away.

"You're finished?" There was surprise in her voice.

"It was filling."

She stood. "I'll take care of the dishes."

"I've got it."

"Let me put the leftovers in a container for your lunch," she offered.

"Okay."

Justin did his thing and she did hers and the whole time she kept up constant chatter about her new family.

"I brought Kyle's pajamas along in case time slipped away. It seems to do that when I'm over there. Michelle helped me give him a bath."

"Oh?"

"Can you believe she still has tub toys from when my brothers were little?" She was at the island and glanced over her shoulder to look at him. "She's saving them for grandchildren."

"So I guess she's looking forward to that."

Emma nodded. "So far she says the boys aren't cooperating, but she continues to hope."

"Optimism is good."

"Can't argue with that." She snapped the lid on the container and walked over to the refrigerator with it. "Kyle is so busy at their house and they love playing with him. But it sure does wear him out."

Partly he was pleased that his son was able to experience yet another social outlet, but a darker part of him wasn't so thrilled. He finished rinsing his dishes then dried his hands. Emma was close enough that he could reach out and touch her, pull her into his arms.

Kiss her.

"They are amazing people," she said. "I'm glad I came here and so grateful for all you did for me."

She moved in front of him and stood on tiptoe to press her lips to his cheek. Quickly, before he could shift and capture her mouth with his the way he planned, she backed up out of reach. The distance she was deliberately putting between them bothered him. And the way she was using past tense—*glad I came here. All you did for me...*

Was she saying goodbye? Preparing to give her notice?

For a short time tonight Justin had seen a glimpse of life without her and it unsettled him. When he'd been married, most nights he was alone while Kristina was out being the toast of Beverly Hills. He'd known her a lot longer and missed her a lot less than he'd missed Emma tonight.

And then there was Kyle. If she disappeared from his life, he was old enough to notice. She'd be gone and he wouldn't understand why. That could leave scars on a kid. Justin had to do something to make sure that didn't happen.

And without thinking it through, he said, "There's something I need to say."

"All right. Shoot." She looked up at him expectantly.

"I think we should get married."

Chapter Thirteen

"I'm sorry?" Emma blinked. "You want to do what now?"

"Get married."

It was on the tip of her tongue to say this is so sudden, but that sounded like something from a bad movie. All she could do was stare.

"Say something, Emma."

"Okay. You asked for it. This is so sudden." She turned away and began to massage her temples. Her head was starting to throb.

"You're right. I'm doing this badly. I'll pour us a glass of wine and we'll talk it through."

"I'd like that." She turned and smiled as hope squeezed through the knot of confused tension coiling through her.

Justin opened the refrigerator and pulled out a bottle of chardonnay. He took a foil cutter and corkscrew from the kitchen drawer and muscled the cork out, making the whole process look like the sexiest thing ever. Then he poured some of the pale yellow liquid into two glasses and picked them up.

"Follow me," he said.

Emma didn't trust herself to speak and simply nodded. She walked behind him into the family room, where he set the wine down on the coffee table. The stemware were side by side, an indication the two of them should sit next to each other, too. She went first and he sat down, so close their thighs brushed. And she still didn't know what to say.

This was big.

She hadn't been at a loss for words since... Come to think of it, the same thing happened when she told her parents who she was. That was big, too. And that started her thinking.

Who was she?

She'd been raised by a woman who wasn't her mother, a woman who'd stolen her away from her family. She'd grown up in a lie. Then her fiancé, the man she'd thought loved her, turned out to be a lying, cheating jerk who slept with other women pretty much the whole time they'd dated.

And now, Justin had said she should marry him. The question had to be asked.

"Why?"

"Why what?" He rested his elbows on his knees.

She stared at the full wineglasses neither of them had touched. "You said we should get married. That came out of nowhere. What's going on?"

"It makes sense."

"Really? To whom?"

"Think about it." He looked at her. "Don't we get along well? We have fun."

"Yes."

That was too true. In and out of bed. Justin made her laugh, something that had gotten her through a really bad time. But what was he proposing? Shouldn't it be more?

"And then there's this. Tell me you don't love my son." An element of challenge crept into his voice.

She met his gaze then. "I can't imagine loving him more if he was mine."

Justin's eyes went from teasing to tormented. "His own mother was too selfish to give up her parties and shopping for her own child. He's lucky to have you."

And the light was beginning to come on. "What is this really about, Justin?"

"You. Me." His movements were a little stiff when he took her hand into his and rested them on his thigh. "It's all working. More than one person has said what a beautiful family we are. Kyle would have a mother and father. We could give him normal."

Something was off; too many steps had been skipped. From the beginning Justin had indicated his goal was to do anything necessary to make his son's life as normal as possible. Anything but fall in love. Marriage without it was how far he was willing to go for his son. That was too far for her.

"As much as I care about Kyle, that's not good enough."

A muscle jerked in his jaw. "We like each other. That's important and a hell of a lot more honest than what I had before. Or what you had."

"And that's the thing. You told me after we, you know…" Had sex was what she was trying to say. Her cheeks burned, but she had to soldier on. "You were very clear that I should understand there was no chance of anything serious between us. You didn't want to lead me on." She looked at their joined hands and pulled hers away. "So I have to ask, Justin. What's changed?"

"It just seems like a good time," he said, not really answering the question.

Emma studied him and didn't think he was deliberately lying, but this wasn't the complete truth. Everything he'd said described the relationship they had and it had been fine until she revealed her true identity to her family. She'd done what she came to Blackwater Lake to do. So...

And then she got it.

Her mission was accomplished and he believed she would go back to her life in California. His life here would be disrupted, and more important, Kyle would be upset. A legal commitment would trump an employment contract and keep her here in Blackwater Lake. But the plan was fundamentally flawed.

He looked down at his feet. "So, I've made my case. What do you say?"

Deep down she'd hoped very hard that he would come up with the right reason to propose marriage. It broke her heart that he hadn't. "There's a problem."

He shook his head. "I don't think so."

"Maybe it's just a problem for me." She straightened and took a deep breath. There would be no taking this back. "You used the wrong L-word."

"You're not making sense."

"It's perfectly clear to me. We *like* each other, that's true. But when I get married, it won't be for convenience. Love is the only reason to take that step."

"So you believe in it." He wasn't asking a question.

"Yes." She stood and moved away as the pain in her heart started to get bigger. "Without love, marriage is nothing but a pretense. My whole life has been a lie. I already had a fake family and I don't want another one."

"That's not what it would be like." He stood, too, and looked down at her.

"You're wrong. A little while ago you talked about doing a procedure to help a wound heal. The thing is, you have a wound inside that you simply refuse to treat. What you're suggesting isn't right for me."

"I'll make it right." He reached for her.

Emma backed away from his touch, not trusting herself to resist him and the offer that was so very wrong. And she suddenly knew without a doubt that she couldn't stay here with him.

Justin wasn't the sort of man who took no for an answer. He would continue to make his case. Where he was concerned, there'd been enough weak moments for her not to know that if one more mistake happened, it would be the biggest one of all.

"I have to go, Justin."

"Of course. You're tired. We'll talk in the morning—"

"No. I mean, I'm leaving. I can't stay here."

Shock darkened his eyes, followed quickly by something that looked a lot like a sense of betrayal. "What about our agreement?"

"I'm sorry for the short notice. We can work something out until you find someone to live in, but I can't stay here in the house with you. Goodbye, Justin."

A short time later, Emma knocked on the door where the Crawfords had said goodbye to her and Kyle just a little while ago. It was now about eight-thirty. Shifting nervously, she kicked herself for not calling ahead, but there'd been a lot on her mind after leaving Justin's. If anyone came to her door at this hour, she'd ask who it is before she opened it. Fortunately, this was Blackwater Lake and only moments passed before Michelle was standing there.

"Emma? What's wrong?"

"Is it all right if I come in?"

"Of course." Without another word the woman stepped back and held an arm out, welcoming her.

She toyed with her keys. "I have a favor to ask and it's completely all right if you want to say no. So be honest—"

"Anything you need. Tell me." She closed the door.

"Would it be all right if I spent the night here with you?" She held up her hand as Michelle opened her mouth. "Before you answer, it will probably be more than one night."

"You can stay with us as long as you want." Michelle looked concerned. "Where's the baby?"

It was a logical question. Every time Emma had been here since revealing the truth at the birthday party, Kyle had been with her. "At the house with his father."

That explained almost nothing, but she was afraid to say more, afraid she would burst into tears. Justin's marriage-of-convenience proposal was still too painful and raw. She'd left the house with her jacket, purse and a whole bunch of confusion.

"Can I make you some tea?"

"That would be nice." Hard liquor would be better, but she didn't share that. For now, she was grateful Michelle wasn't pushing for details.

They walked through the house's dim interior and Michelle flipped on the kitchen light as she entered the room. Emma sat on a barstool at the black granite island separating the food-preparation area from the family room. The sink was to her left with a window above it, and she faced the stove topped by a stainless-steel microwave. An eating nook was on her right.

It was a homey room with a white baker's rack holding cookbooks and knickknacks. There were pictures everywhere. Suspended from the ceiling was a copper rack where pots and pans hung. Behind her, a flat-screen TV was mounted on the wall with a sofa and chair grouped around it. The furniture was conspicuously empty.

"Where's Alan?" she asked.

"Out with the boys for some male bonding while they're in town. I'm quite certain that beer and a pool table will be involved."

"Sounds fun," Emma commented.

"I'm sure they think so." She took an orange teapot on top of the stove and filled it with water from the faucet at the sink. Then she set it on a front burner and turned on the gas. "Frankly, this house is way too quiet with them gone. It's really nice to have female company, and you're actually doing me a favor being here."

"I'm glad."

Emma had been so upset on her way out of Justin's house it had slipped her mind that her brothers were here. "Are you sure there's room for me to stay? I didn't think about the guys being here."

"Pierce and Zach are checked in at Blackwater Lake Lodge. Only Kane is here"

While she talked, Michelle took mugs from an upper cupboard, then opened a canister on the counter and pulled out two tea bags. She held them up so Emma could see what kind and she nodded her approval of Sleepytime. It was doubtful that would live up to its name, but maybe the warm drink would do something about the cold inside her.

"So," Michelle continued, "I don't want to hear another word about putting anyone out."

Emma was pretty sure the other woman *did* want to hear words about why she'd asked for asylum so suddenly at night. That was something she wasn't ready to discuss. At the same time, she had to admire Michelle for her restraint. Not many women could hold back the questions she must have. It was very much appreciated because Emma needed to get her emotions under control first.

For the past year she'd been trying to figure out who she really was. Since she'd become nanny to his son, Justin had been there for her and now she was reeling because he'd asked her to marry him when he clearly didn't love her.

Despite all that confusion, one thing was crystal clear.

From the moment Michelle opened the door to her, she'd felt safe. For now she'd rock that feeling. She was procrastinating again but decided to cut herself some slack.

The teakettle whistled and Michelle turned off the burner then poured water into two tall mugs. She pushed the green one over to Emma and wrapped her hands around the orange one before walking to the other side of the island and taking the tall stool next to Emma.

She blew on the steaming liquid then said, "So, Thanksgiving is this Thursday."

Obviously the woman had picked what should have been a neutral subject, but Emma's heart hurt thinking about the upcoming holiday. She'd been so looking forward to fixing dinner for Justin and Kyle, to spending the day with them. That wasn't happening now. Why couldn't he have left everything alone?

Michelle filled the silence. "Seems like thirty seconds ago it was summer and now it will be Christmas before you know it."

"I love this time of year," Emma felt obliged to comment, and truth was always best. "The tree. Lights everywhere. Santa Claus and shopping."

"Did you believe in Santa?" It was clear the other woman put a lot of effort into keeping her tone neutral, but her smile was strained around the edges.

"I still believe." The smile lost a little of the strain and made Emma glad her words were light. "No one told me he wasn't real, so I'm keeping the magic alive."

"Good for you. Kane is thirty-two years old and I think he still holds a grudge against Zach for spilling the beans. They were eight and four when that particular Christmas magic died a painful death."

Emma experienced a wave of profound sadness. A Christmas crisis that had turned into a warm family memory had been stolen from her. All she could do was hear about it. "Why would he do that?"

Michelle laughed. "Alan and I took the boys to see Santa on Christmas Eve. The three of them were just too excited to be still, and channeling the energy seemed like a good idea at the time. Then Zach sat on Santa's knee and told him something that he wanted and hadn't shared with us."

"What was it?"

Michelle shook her head. "I can't even remember. But it was too late to shop. Needless to say, the item wasn't under the tree the next morning. Also needless to say, he wasn't a happy camper, and to salvage the day, his father and I decided it was time to tell him the truth." She shrugged. "The next thing we knew, he'd decided to share the information with his younger brothers."

"Once it's out of the bag, there's no way to put it back inside."

"Isn't that the truth. We wanted to strangle him." She smiled fondly at the memory. "At least one of our children still believes."

The youngest of Emma's brothers was four years older than she was. She'd have been too young to have the secret spoiled. What she'd said about still believing in Santa Claus had been the right thing to say and she was pleased.

"I'm glad you're glad." Emma took a sip of her tea and holidays through the years flashed through her mind. All the memories and milestones a mother would have missed. She felt a responsibility to somehow make it up. "You know, I have an album of pictures you might like to see. It's a collection of photos of me that my mother—"

The other woman was just lifting the mug and her hand jerked, spilling the hot liquid. "Darn it. That was clumsy."

She set it down and slid off the stool then hurried to the sink and a roll of paper towels on a holder beside it. Emma didn't know what to do or say. She shouldn't have called the woman who'd kidnapped her "mother" in front of the one who'd given birth to her. It was a stupid mistake but habits were hard to break.

"I'm sorry."

Those two words probably didn't help, but what else could she say? The truth was out and tests had been done, proving she was who she claimed to be. They'd notified the police, who had closed the long-open missing child case. All should have been right, but it wasn't. The wounds were still open and raw.

Michelle finally looked at her. "It's all right."

"I hope you know that I'd never purposely say or do anything to upset you."

"I know. It's just…" She pressed her lips together and shook her head. "Never mind."

Emma slid off the stool. "Seriously, that was thoughtless and I—"

"Forget it." Michelle threw wet paper towels in the trash then looked at the digital clock on the microwave. "You must be tired. Are your things in the car?"

"No. I didn't pack a bag."

"I see." Clearly she didn't, because questions and concern swirled in her eyes. "Well, I'll find something for you to sleep in and we'll worry about the rest in the morning. How's that?"

"Thank you." Emma meant that in so many ways.

Michelle was being awfully gracious in spite of that distressing slip of the tongue. Emma wanted her words back in the worst way. It was ironic really. She'd barely finished saying, in reference to the Santa incident, that once something is out of the bag, there's no way to put it back. How she'd wished to be wrong.

Neither of them said anything as they walked upstairs. Michelle opened the door to a room with an adjoining bath.

"The sheets are clean. I always make up the beds right away after the boys are here because they have a habit of dropping in without warning."

"Since I dropped in unannounced tonight, it appears that's another inherited tendency."

"I guess so." The other woman smiled a little. "I'll just get you something to sleep in."

"Thanks."

Alone, Emma looked around the room. There was a queen-size bed covered with a floral comforter in shades of pink and green. Across from the bed was a dressing table with a needlepoint rose on the cushion of the chair in front of it. There were pictures on the walls and three of them were coordinating prints. One was a little girl eating an apple while reading a book. Underneath, it said Fairy Tales. The second was a girl with a paintbrush stuck in a top-of-the-head ponytail captioned Budding Genius. Last was a character that looked like Cinderella, complete with poofy blue dress and cameo choker. It said, Little Princess.

This room had not been decorated with one of her brothers in mind.

There was a quick knock on the door. "Emma?"

"Yes." She whirled around.

"Here you go." Michelle set a pair of black-and-white flannel pajamas and a fuzzy pink robe on the bed. "We're about the same height, so those should fit. They might be a little big."

"I'm sure they'll be fine. Thanks so much."

"You're welcome." She edged out the door. "If you need anything, just ask."

"I will. I really appreciate this."

"Sleep tight."

Then Emma was alone and felt like slime for what she'd said. She wished Michelle would talk about it. This felt wrong and awful just when she'd thought at least part of her life was falling into place.

In the bathroom she washed up as best she could without her own toiletries and changed into the borrowed sleepwear. She'd just climbed into bed when there was another knock.

Emma turned the switch on the lamp beside the bed, bathing the area in soft light. "Come in."

Michelle opened the door. "I forgot to tell you. If you get cold, there are extra blankets in the closet."

"Okay." She hesitated, then decided what the heck. "Can we talk?"

"Of course." The other woman walked over to the bed and sat down at the foot. "What's on your mind?"

"What I said before. In the kitchen…" She picked at the soft green blanket. "I didn't mean to hurt you. I hope you know I would never do that on purpose."

"I know."

"It's part of the reason I was so conflicted about whether or not to tell you who I am." She blew out a breath. "I know she took me. I get that, but—"

"I was shopping." Michelle had a look on her face as if she had gone back in time and was in that horrible moment. "You were in the stroller. Six weeks old. Just an infant. The beautiful little girl Alan and I had wished for after three boys. It's no excuse, but I was so tired. I stopped in an aisle that was very close to the exit door and picked up a jar. It slipped out of my hand and broke. Pickles and juice went everywhere. I was embarrassed and distracted, trying to let an employee know about the mess so no one would slip and get hurt. It seemed only a moment, but when I turned back, you and the stroller were gone."

The haunted expression had Emma sliding forward to grip her hand. "I can't even imagine how that felt."

"No one saw anything. You just disappeared. There was so much confusion, searching the store. By the time what really happened sank in, she was long gone with you."

"That must have been awful."

"An understatement." She looked around the room. "Eventually we had to put your baby things away, but your father and I always hoped you were alive and would come home someday."

"So this room was mine." It wasn't a question.

The other woman smiled. "Yes."

"It's beautiful." Emma bit her lip, trying to figure out how to say this right. "The thing is, she did a bad thing and intellectually I know that. But she wasn't mean or a bad person. She raised me, she was kind and loving. I thought she was my mother. That's how I think of her, although now I'm also angry and confused. It will take a while for all of this to sink in."

"Understandable."

"But if that hurts you or makes you uncomfortable, I can leave—"

"No. Don't even say that. The situation is bewildering and will take some getting used to, but we'll get through this." She smoothed the blanket more securely over Emma's legs, then patted her knee. "Happy doesn't even begin to describe how I feel at having you back. I'll never recover the memories and experiences that were stolen and, I have to be honest, I'm not sure I'll ever forgive her for robbing me of that."

"Her name was Ruth."

Michelle nodded. "Your father and I named you Sarah Elizabeth after both of your grandmothers."

"I'm not sure what to say, except it's a nice name, but for me it's surreal."

"I just wanted you to know. I hadn't even thought about the legal ramifications because there's a birth certificate, but obviously she, Ruth, managed to do what was necessary to enroll you in school and anything else you'd need legal documentation for."

"I don't remember any problem with it. Obviously it was forged."

"Well, we've hired an attorney to figure this all out. But, for now, I feel incredibly lucky to have you here."

Emma smiled. "Me, too. I thought I was all alone."

"Never." She nodded firmly. "You're stuck with us now."

"Speaking of that…" She met the other woman's gaze. "I don't even know what to call you and Alan."

"You can call me Michelle. Hey, you. Or anything else you'd like."

Emma smiled and slid forward to hug the other woman. "How about Mom?"

Maternal arms tightened around her. "That works for me."

"Me, too—" Her voice broke.

Her mother held on for several moments, then took Emma's face between her hands. "I'm glad we had this talk."

"I am, too."

"Now you need to get some rest."

"Good night, Mom."

"Sleep tight, daughter." She stood and smiled. "I finally will sleep well now that my baby girl is back home."

When Emma was alone, thoughts of Justin popped into her mind. And Kyle. She wouldn't be there in the morning and his careful routine would be completely messed up. He wouldn't understand what was happening and that made her feel horrible.

But Justin was there and he'd take care of the little guy until she could figure out what to do so that baby boy didn't feel abandoned.

So much for sleeping.

Chapter Fourteen

The next morning Emma had the vague, sleepy impression of being in an unfamiliar place and opening her eyes confirmed it. This pretty room was different and there was no baby chatter to greet her. Everything came back in a rush, including Justin's proposal. There was nothing vague and sleepy about the pain that squeezed her heart. She missed Kyle terribly and wondered if he missed her, too.

It was Saturday and Mercy Medical Clinic was closed, so Justin wouldn't need her today. But she couldn't leave him hanging and would call later. During a sleepless night she'd decided to make a proposal of her own. Child care without living in his house.

She'd arrive before he left for work and leave when he got home, but only until he found someone to replace her. If he had an emergency during the night, she would come over and stay with Kyle. That was the best she could do. What he'd suggested was unacceptable to her.

She smelled coffee and had the pitiful, pathetic thought that it was just what the doctor ordered. Spotting the borrowed pink fuzzy robe still on the end of the bed, she got up and put it on. When she opened the bedroom door voices drifted to her and she followed the sound to the kitchen. Her brother Kane was sitting on the stool where she'd had tea the night before.

He was very handsome, all of her brothers were, but his rumpled, early-morning scruffy look was incredibly appealing. His dark brown hair was cut conservatively short and his blue eyes were full of the devil.

Their mother poured a mug of coffee and set it on the island in front of him. She moved through the doorway and they both looked at her.

"Good morning," she said, taking the stool beside Kane's.

"Morning, sis. Want coffee?"

"More than you can imagine."

He slid his mug in front of her. "Cream and sugar?"

"Cream, and if there's any low-calorie sweetener that would be great."

"Of course there is," her mother said. "What kind of B and B do you think I run here?"

Emma smiled when all the coffee stuff magically appeared in front of her. "Careful. You'll spoil me."

"Good. I have a lot of years to make up for."

Kane's grin was all big-brother wickedness. "Does that mean I get a free pass to pick on her?"

"Not if you want breakfast, young man." She gave him a mom look designed to put a boy in his place. "Speaking of that, what sounds good? Pancakes? Omelets? Crepes?"

"I don't care. Whatever is easy. Please don't go to any trouble." Emma wasn't particularly hungry.

Her brother gave her a "what?" look. "You're missing an opportunity here. This is going to wear off and you've got to work it while you can." He leaned close and whispered loud enough for people in the next county to hear, "Say omelets."

"That's *your* favorite," his mother said. "I asked what Emma wants."

"Omelets would be wonderful. If it's not too much trouble," she added.

"It's not."

Michelle assembled the eggs, cheese, mushrooms, onions, tomatoes and cooking utensils. Her brother got off his stool and refilled all their cups with coffee.

Emma realized her father wasn't there. "Where's Alan? I mean Dad."

"At the diner." Kane had noticed the slip and for just a moment there was a sympathetic look in his eyes. "Saturday mornings are traditionally busy or he wouldn't have gone."

Her mother stopped stirring the eggs in the bowl. "I'm here and not at work because we agreed that this was where I should be this morning. He'll be home as soon as he can, so there's no need for you to feel guilty."

"Too late," she said. "You really don't need to fuss over me—"

"Yes, I do. For all these years I couldn't be with you when you needed me, but now I can. And something is definitely going on. We'll get to it. But first I'm going to cook for my two youngest kids."

"She makes really good omelets," her brother said.

"I hope so or that means you've got really bad taste, brother."

"Okay, you saw that, right Mom? She drew first blood. The gloves come off. Watch your back." He grinned, then glanced at what his mother was doing. "What about fried potatoes?"

"If you want them, get over here and help."

"What about me?" Emma asked. "I want to help, too."

"Why don't you set the table, sweetheart."

"I can do that."

When her mom pointed out where everything was, she did just that. Soon they were seated at the round oak table in the nook. White shutters covered the window, but they were open, and the towering Montana mountains were visible in the distance. Three mugs had been filled with coffee and each of them had a full plate of food.

"This smells wonderful," Emma said.

"Tastes even better." Kane shoveled in another bite.

She watched in awe as he seemed to inhale everything. "How can you eat so much?"

"It's a guy thing."

Emma managed to get down half the omelet and a few potatoes, but the knot in her stomach stopped her from eating it all. "That was delicious."

"You're finished?" Her brother looked doubtful.

"It's a girl thing." She grinned at him. "And you should know that."

"Why?"

"You're a nice-looking guy. Don't you date?"

"The better question," their mother chimed in, "is when does he find time to work."

"So, you have a flourishing social life." Emma wrapped her hands around her mug and met his gaze. "But you're not married. Why is that?"

"Good question." Michelle set her fork on the plate and joined Emma in staring at the token male. "I'd like to know the answer to that, too."

"No fair." Kane squirmed and scowled good-naturedly. "My long-lost sister is back and ganging up on me?"

"What are sisters for?" She grinned at him.

"How come *you're* not married?" His plate was clean and he pushed it away.

"Because I was engaged to a guy who I discovered had been cheating on me the whole time we were dating." Emma found that it didn't bother her at all. She could actually joke about the fiasco that was her fiancé.

"Weasel." Kane's blue eyes narrowed a little dangerously. "I'll beat him up for you."

"Okay." She rested her forearms on the table. "I always wanted a big brother to do stuff like that."

"Now you've got three," he promised.

"So, is there a guy here in Blackwater Lake who needs a visit from the Crawford brothers?" Her mother's brown eyes had a knowing glint.

"You want to know why I'm here." Emma knew it didn't take a mental giant to figure out her sudden appearance last night had something to do with a man.

Her mother squeezed her hand. "It's time to confess why you ran away from Justin."

"Do I have to?"

"You'll feel better." Kane looked at his mother when she laughed. "What? That's what you always tell me."

"For all the good it does." She sighed. "You never talk to me about anything. I'm hoping Emma will."

"Wow, the honeymoon is over," Emma joked. Then the humor faded. "I showed up on your doorstep last night and you didn't hesitate to take me in. More important, you didn't ask any questions. I appreciate that. And you have a right to know what's going on."

"I notice you didn't include me in that," her brother commented.

"You weren't here. The Crawford male-bonding ritual was more important."

"Mom told you." He shrugged. "I'm here now. And you

should know I'm not leaving. Just in case you change your mind and need some muscle."

"Good to know." She smiled. "The thing is, I can't live with Justin anymore."

"I knew it." Kane's expression was two parts gotcha and one part anger. "He made a move on you."

He'd done more than that, but she'd been an eager accomplice. "He asked me to marry him."

Kane stared at her for several moments then said, "I'm not sure what to say. Do you want me to take him out back and beat the crap out of him?"

"You don't understand—"

"Ignore your brother, sweetheart. Take your time."

"Thanks, Mom." Emma sighed, remembering that sinking sensation when that oh-wow-he-cares feeling changed because his real intentions became clear. "He was proposing a marriage of convenience."

"Why?" Kane's tone was full of bewilderment.

"He wants guaranteed child care for his son."

"But not an emotional connection," her mother finished.

"Exactly. The thing is, he was married before and it didn't go well." The details weren't Emma's to share. "But he won't let himself care because love let him down in a big way."

"Okay." Kane nodded. "So he has his reasons."

"Now whose side are you on?" Emma asked.

"Mine." He stood and picked up his empty plate. "This is where you guys get into the mushy stuff and there's nothing I can add. So, I'm out of here."

He put his plate in the sink before leaving the room.

"Men." Michelle sighed. "They're good for opening stubborn mayonnaise jars and changing a tire. But when it comes to touchy-feely issues they're not much help."

"So much for the male point of view," Emma agreed.

Her mother looked thoughtful. "Justin was serious about getting married?"

"I'm sure he was. And it's weird because at my first interview he made it clear that he wasn't looking for a wife." It was practically the first thing he'd said. "So it was a shock when he brought it up out of the blue. If he wasn't prepared to follow through, why would he have asked?"

"I think he's serious. I mean, serious feelings," her mother clarified.

"Not possible." In his bed he'd told her not to get the wrong idea, although that wasn't something she was prepared to reveal.

"He might not want to have them, but a man doesn't get to the point of asking what he asked without deep emotion to back it up." Her mother's expression turned tender. "But I'm more concerned about you. How do you feel about him?"

Surprisingly, Emma didn't hesitate. The truth had been in her heart for a while but she'd refused to acknowledge it. "I love him," she said simply.

She was certain of it. He was a good man, a good father. And he would be a good husband if he'd let himself. But he'd given no indication of changing his mind about that.

"Emma, you have to face this head-on. Hiding isn't the answer and running away won't help."

"You're right." As difficult and awful as it would be, she needed to explain to Justin the reason she'd left. "But I don't think you're right about his feelings for me."

"Maybe not. But you won't know unless you face him. And take it from me, knowing is better."

Emma knew she wasn't just talking about the situation with Justin. Her mother had lived in limbo for so many years and still had the courage to put one foot in front of the other. She was the best kind of role model.

"I need to get my clothes," she said.

"Your brother will go."

"Doesn't that make me a coward?" Emma asked.

"No. You need your own things before you have that conversation with Justin." Her mother smiled. "A girl needs to look her best."

"I'm so glad you get it." Emma stood, then leaned down to hug the other woman.

"My first mother-daughter talk." Brown eyes so like her own glistened and her mom sniffled. "How did I do?"

"Pretty terrific."

And her family was pretty awesome, too. On this journey of self-discovery Emma had worried about where she belonged. How ironic that she'd found her place and lost her heart at the same time.

And nowhere in the law of karma did it say that life would let you have it all.

Justin was relieved when Camille Halliday opened her door, even though he'd called to say he was coming over. She and Ben McKnight lived a couple miles from his house and he needed a friend to talk to. He also thought a woman's touch might help calm Kyle. The baby had been out of sorts since waking up that morning and seeing him instead of his nanny.

"Emma's gone."

"What do you mean, gone?"

"She left last night and Kyle's fussy. He's not taking it well. And you're a woman."

The little boy took one look at her and let out a wail, then buried his face in Justin's neck.

Cam rubbed a hand over her pregnant belly. "I'm definitely a woman, but not the one he wants."

"It was worth a try."

Justin didn't like this. He didn't like curveballs. His

approach to life was planning and execution. Normally it was a win-win. Not this time. He'd acted spontaneously, made his pitch and everything fell apart.

"Come inside, Justin. You look terrible."

"Thanks." He walked past her and she closed the door. "For letting me in, not the making-fun-of-me part."

Sleepless nights were nothing new. During med school, internship, residency and private practice, a doctor often didn't get eight straight hours and frequently pulled an all-nighter. But that was professional. An employee walking out should have been, too. If Ginny quit her job at Mercy Medical Clinic, it would be inconvenient, but manageable. Emma leaving felt damn personal *and* unmanageable.

"I'll put on some coffee."

"Where's Ben?"

"Shopping. I think he's bringing home a surprise for the baby." She smiled. "A glider chair. So actually it's for me. And not really a surprise."

Cam headed to the back of the house where the large kitchen and family room combination had an entire wall of windows. There was an incredible view of the mountains, and normally the beauty had a calming effect, but not today.

Carrying Kyle, Justin walked over to the black granite-covered island as big as an aircraft carrier. There were green glass jars with delicate lids and a statue of a skinny French chef. A napkin holder beside crystal salt-and-pepper shakers finished off the knickknack grouping. Everything was breakable and his son wanted it all. He let out a frustrated cry when Justin pushed the things out of reach.

"Sorry, pal. Those aren't toys."

Cam pressed the button on the coffeemaker and instantly a sizzling sound filled the room. "Did you bring anything for him to play with?"

"Not unless there's something in the diaper bag." He lifted a shoulder where it was hanging.

"So you didn't pack it."

"No. Emma always took care of that."

"I don't have any toys yet." Cam moved her palm over her baby bump while she thought for a moment. "But I've got an idea."

In the kitchen she grabbed wooden spoons out of a crockery jar on the counter, opened a drawer and pulled out plastic measuring cups, then gathered nonbreakable leftover containers and lids. She carried it all to the family room and put it on the floor.

"Set him down. This might be a distraction because everything is unfamiliar to him."

The boy watched her with interest then made a grunting sound and reached out for the new stuff. After he was settled on the plush carpet, the first thing he picked up was a spoon. The first thing he did was whack one of the bowls.

"Good idea, Cam. He can't make too much noise banging on plastic."

She poured coffee into a mug, got herself a glass of water then awkwardly settled herself on a high stool that faced the family room. "So, what happened with Emma? You said she was gone. Where did she go?"

"To her parents'." Everyone in town knew that the Crawfords had their daughter back. "She called earlier to say she would watch Kyle during the day until I can find a replacement for her."

And that ticked him off. How was he supposed to do that? A daunting prospect would be climbing Mount Everest, but replacing Emma would take a miracle.

"That doesn't sound like she's gone, as in really *gone,*" Cam commented.

Justin sat on the edge of the floral-covered sofa, close to where Kyle was busily slapping a green-and-white measuring cup on the rug. "How about this, then? Her brother Kane came over for her clothes and things."

The guy hadn't said much but was clearly protective. He hadn't been at the house long, but when he left with her packed suitcase, Justin's anger melted, releasing something that felt a lot like pain. If a doctor knew anything, it was that pain was an indicator of something very wrong.

"Let me get this straight." She tapped a finger on the granite. "She didn't leave you high and dry as far as child care is concerned."

That's not how it felt. His son's routine had been thrown into chaos and that was unacceptable.

"Kyle really feels her absence."

Cam smiled tenderly at the little boy chattering away to all the things around him. Then she met Justin's gaze and there was a knowing look in her eyes. He wasn't particularly fond of the expression women wore when they became aware of something a man couldn't seem to comprehend on his own.

"Kyle isn't the only one not taking this well."

"If you're talking about me, that's just wrong. I'm doing fine, if you don't count the part where household routine is turned on its ass."

"No, you're not upset at all."

"A grown man isn't allowed to be fussy," he said.

"Just crabby," she retorted.

"I'm not—" The look she aimed at him said protesting was a waste of breath. "Okay. Maybe a little."

"So...cool, calm, collected Dr. Flint is hot under the collar. That's clear evidence this is more than your nanny giving notice. Emma *put* you on notice by leaving. Spill it, Justin. Confession is good for the soul. What really happened to send her packing?"

He blew out a breath and weighed the pros and cons of telling her, then realized he had nothing to lose. "I asked her to marry me."

Cam's expression went from surprised to pleased. Then she frowned. "If that had gone well, you wouldn't be here in a snit and she wouldn't be staying at her parents'. What did you say to her?"

"We like each other. We have fun together. Marriage makes sense."

"Obviously not to her." Cam's eyes narrowed. "What else did you say?"

"I reminded her that she loves Kyle. He's lucky to have her. If she agreed to marry me, he would have a mother and father. We could give him a normal life."

And that was when Emma had reminded him of his own warning that he wasn't looking for a wife. He'd said what he'd said because he wanted to be up front with her. Look how well that turned out. Being honest had blown up in his face.

And speaking of faces…Cam's disapproving look made him want to squirm, but he held it together. She didn't need to know that Emma had called him out on using the wrong L-word.

"You didn't tell her you love her." So much for Cam not knowing. "Look, Justin, you didn't come here because taking care of your son is a challenge for you. When he was an infant and his mother was off doing whatever it was she did, you handled that little guy like a pro."

"Thank you."

"I'm not finished." Cam slid off the stool. "Next to my fiancé, you're the most honorable man I know, so don't start lying to me now. You came here because I'm your friend and you needed someone to talk sense into you. This reaction of yours is more than just to an employee quitting."

The words struck a chord, but he didn't like the tone he got. "If you're saying what I think you are, that's not a place I'm prepared to go again."

"Sometimes our head goes in one direction," she said more gently, "and the heart goes somewhere else, whether or not we want it to."

"You're trying to say I have feelings for her?"

Cam nodded like a teacher proud of the star pupil. "Any idiot can see that you're head over heels in love with her."

Justin's mind was racing at the same time he carefully watched Kyle push to his feet and toddle around the family room. A leather ottoman doubled as a coffee table, so no sharp corners or breakable stuff there. On short, chubby legs the little boy checked things out, then tottered over to Cam. She smiled but stayed still and let him get used to her.

"Can I give him a cookie?" she asked. "Vanilla wafer. Ben likes them, but I think it should be age appropriate for Kyle. I've been reading up on all the stages."

"He'd like that."

She moved to the pantry and the little boy followed her. He was right there when she pulled out the box. After squatting to his level, she reached in and took out a cookie for him. He grinned and snatched it away then said two unintelligible syllables that sounded a little like "thank you."

Cam's expression turned soft and tender. "Good to know food is a bridge to détente."

"You're a terrific friend. And you'll be an even more terrific mom," Justin said.

"Like Emma." She met his gaze. "That woman has set a very high bar."

"She's awfully good with him. It's obvious he misses her." Justin heard the longing in his own voice.

"You know how I felt about Kristina. Your wife was a schemer, and I never minced words to you about that, right?"

"I remember."

"Obviously I'm willing to hit you with the truth on bad stuff, so my opinion should count for something." At his nod, she continued. "I'm telling you that Emma is the real deal. She's a keeper and you know it in your gut. Trust your instincts."

"Because they've never let me down," he said wryly.

Cam put her arm around the little boy who was digging his little hand in the box for another cookie. "I understand why you're feeling snarky right now, but get over it. If you don't fix this with Emma, you'll be in big trouble."

Again the words struck a chord and Justin realized she wasn't wrong about that. The question was *how* to fix it when he'd made such a mess of everything.

Chapter Fifteen

Justin liked having a plan.

He was a surgeon and before picking up a scalpel, he studied notes and photos, went through each step of the procedure in his mind. By the time he'd scrubbed in, he knew exactly where to make the incision and how much pressure to apply so that every cut was as shallow as possible. Do No Harm was the cornerstone of medical practice, but when intervention was necessary it was a doctor's responsibility to do the least amount of damage possible to the body.

So he had a plan in place when he pulled the SUV to a stop at the curb in front of the Crawfords' house. After turning off the ignition, he ticked off in his mind what he would say to Emma.

Apologize for being insensitive.

Be honest with her about his feelings. He didn't like labels and that's what had landed him in trouble. The primary message he had to convey was that he cared for her deeply. After everything that had happened to her, she would appreciate truthfulness and integrity.

Finally, he would ask her to come home because he and Kyle missed her. His son just wasn't his usual cheerful self and clearly felt the change. Fortunately, Cam and Ben had offered to keep him while Justin convinced Emma to come back.

The sun was just disappearing behind the mountains as he exited the car and walked up the path to the door. It was opened almost immediately after he rang the doorbell.

"Hello, Justin."

"Sir."

Wow, he hadn't planned to say that. He'd been on a first-name basis with Alan Crawford since they'd met. But that was before Emma had started work as his son's nanny. Now everyone in town knew that this man was her father. And Justin was here because he'd slept with the man's daughter. That was sort of what was on his mind. Mostly he wanted her back in whatever way she would have him.

His plan had only included talking to Emma, but her father was the one standing there, a big clue that he hadn't thought this through. And then her brothers appeared behind Alan in the doorway. Justin had met them at their mother's birthday party, the night Emma had revealed her identity.

Kane, the youngest and the guy who'd packed her suitcase, stood directly behind their father and was about an inch taller. Middle brother, Pierce, was to the left. His hair was a shade darker than the other two and his light blue eyes had a challenge in them. This wasn't the time to let him know there was a procedure that could minimize the scar on his chin.

Rounding out the foursome was Zach, the oldest. He had brown eyes like Emma and his mother, but there wasn't an ounce of warmth in them. He was taller and broader through the shoulders than the other three, a rugged man who obviously worked hard.

The family was running interference for Emma and that was not part of his plan.

"Nice to see you all again."

"What do you want, Justin?" Alan did the talking, but the other three listened intently.

"I'm here to talk to Emma."

"Why?" Zach wanted to know.

"It's between the two of us."

Alan shook his head. "She's not alone anymore. Whatever is on your mind, you can say it in front of her family."

"Isn't that for her to decide?" Justin was pretty sure she wouldn't want their personal details made public. He sure didn't, and this inquisition was starting to tick him off. "Will you tell her I'm here to speak with her? Please."

"I'm not sure she even wants to see you." It was strange, but Kane's expression had just a touch of empathy. His voice wasn't quite as dangerous as her father's and oldest brother's. "According to what she told me, she can't be your live-in nanny anymore."

"That sounds final to me," Zach commented.

Pierce moved slightly closer to his father, making the four men a solid, united front. "She knows her own mind."

"And you're aware of this how?" Justin said. "You've known her for what? Thirty seconds?"

Alan's mouth pulled tight for a moment. "She's my daughter. A father has an instinct about his child and she's a strong, resilient woman. No one is going to push her around."

Anger rolled through Justin at the thought of anyone doing that to Emma. He blew out a long breath and said, "I'm not a bully."

"She never said you were." Kane rubbed a big hand

across his neck. "You've got your reasons for not being all in for whatever it is between the two of you. All of us—Pierce, Zach and me—we've all been where you are. But when it's over, it's over."

"Did she say it was over?" Justin rejected that with everything he had. It couldn't be over. The idea of her not being in his life was what had pushed him into the stupid things he'd said.

"What part of 'she can't be your nanny anymore' did you not understand?" Zach didn't exactly move forward but seemed to block his way more aggressively. "Maybe it's time for you to move on, Doctor."

"When Emma said what she said, there were things she didn't know about." That was all he was prepared to say. He met Alan's gaze because the man was her father and deserved the respect.

"What are your intentions toward my daughter?"

This was starting to feel like the Old West and any second he expected them to pull six-guns. Justin was pretty sure not many fathers in Beverly Hills asked that question. She was an adult, a smart, beautiful woman who could take care of herself. The reality was that *he* wanted to take care of her. Those angry words were a nanosecond from coming out of his mouth, when thoughts of Kyle popped into his mind.

If anyone hurt his son, Justin would be acting like the Crawfords. He owed her father the courtesy of reassurance that there was no way he would hurt or dishonor Emma.

"I already asked her to marry me."

"That's true," Kane confirmed. "She told Mom and me this morning."

"But she obviously said no." Pierce looked at his brothers. "So, I don't get why he's here."

"Married once," Kane said. "Wasn't good."

Zach nodded. "So, he's got reasons. Understood. But the question was asked and answered, so it doesn't seem like there's more to say."

Justin wasn't sure what bugged him more—the fact they wouldn't let him pass or that they talked as if he wasn't even there. "Trust me. There's a lot more."

"What?" Alan demanded.

"Look—" His reserves of patience were nearly gone. He was ready to break through this defensive line, but common sense stopped him. Alan was older, but his sons were in their prime. It was four to one, not good odds. "She obviously talked to you about what happened between us. When I've said my piece, if Emma wants you to know, she'll tell you."

Alan stared him down. "You hurt her once already in the last twenty-four hours. When she was stolen from me as a baby, the hardest thing was not being able to protect my little girl. I've got her back now and it's my intention to make sure no harm comes to her ever again and that includes you. Unless there's something you can say to convince me that she won't be hurt, you're not getting through us."

The other three men nodded and Justin knew they were determined. So was he. The need to see Emma was driving him crazy.

"All right." He looked from one man to the next then settled his gaze on Alan. "I think I love her."

"You think?" The other man stared at him for several moments, his eyes narrowing as the seconds ticked by. "Come back when you're sure."

Then the door slammed in his face.

Justin blinked at the solid wood. He wouldn't have been more shocked if Alan had punched him. Or pulled out a six-shooter.

Emma heard the door slam as she walked downstairs holding a magazine. An actual book would have required too much concentration. At least the magazine had pictures. Every time she tried to read a story with a plot, her mind wandered back to her last conversation with Justin. She wanted a do-over more than almost anything she could think of.

She reached the bottom of the stairs where her father and brothers were gathered just inside the door. All four of them were looking at her funny.

"I heard the doorbell a few minutes ago. Who was it?" she asked.

The four men exchanged what could only be described as guilty glances. Boys got bigger and became men, but they never outgrew the look they wore after doing something naughty.

She walked past each of them like a general inspecting the troops. "What's going on?"

"Nothing." Kane rocked back on his heels.

"Why don't I believe you?" She stood in front of Zach, a big, handsome man who would make any woman he cared for feel safe and protected. And she got the feeling that somehow he was protecting her. She appreciated the effort, but her curiosity was really humming now. "What about you? Want to tell me what's going on?"

"Why would you think anything is?" He shifted his feet on the wood floor and squirmed just a little. It was proof that the bigger they were, the harder they fell.

"Because you responded to a question with a question and didn't really answer what I asked. In nanny school I learned that's a classic avoidance technique."

"You went to nanny school?" Pierce asked. "Is that like Mary Poppins University?"

She moved in front of him and couldn't help thinking

she had the hunkiest brothers on the planet. They got even cuter when put on the spot. Why was it none of them were married, engaged or currently dating? That was a question for another day. Right now there was a conspiracy in progress and she would get to the bottom of it.

"The three of you are covering for each other."

"What makes you think that?" Kane did his level best to look innocent and failed completely.

"I know so because Pierce just created a diversion. And, for the record, it didn't work. But obviously someone was about to break and confess." She looked at her father. "You'll tell me the truth, right, Dad?"

"Honey—" One word in a tone that said, don't make me do that.

"I know parents walk a fine line in terms of telling the truth, what with the Tooth Fairy, Easter Bunny and Santa Claus. Technically, letting kids believe mythical characters are real is lying. But when that kid grows up, she can handle the truth. I'm all grown up. Now, who was at the door?"

Alan looked at his sons and shrugged. "She's just like her mother."

"I noticed," Zach said. "But you're stronger than this. Don't give in, Dad."

"I don't know how she knows something is up, but she does. And, like her mother, I suspect she won't let go of this until she gets what she wants."

"Dad, you're stalling," she said.

"Yes, I am," he admitted. Then his face softened. "Justin stopped by."

Emma didn't know why that surprised her. Maybe because he'd been so abrupt and distant on the phone earlier. "What did he say?"

"He wanted to talk to you."

"So, where is he?" She glanced around and could see

into the living room and dining room from this vantage point. She was about to go to the kitchen when it sank in that her father had used the past tense. Her gaze touched on each of her brothers. "No one let me know he was here."

"And there's a good reason for that." Kane looked at his oldest brother. "Tell her what it is, Zach."

His expression said he was very unhappy to have been put on the spot, but Zach squared his broad shoulders. "We wanted to make sure you weren't hurt."

"And just how do you propose to do that?"

"Dad asked him what his intentions are." Pierce obviously was aware that the front line had been breached and was singing like a canary.

Emma stared at her father. "Tell me you didn't really do that."

"I certainly did." He slid his fingertips into the pockets of his jeans. "And I'd do it again. For my sons, too, if it ever becomes necessary."

That was heartwarming and annoying in equal parts. She was going to hate herself, but had to ask. "What did he say?"

"At first nothing, but he could see we wouldn't back down." Zach looked extraordinarily pleased at standing their ground.

"At first? That means he said something eventually and I'd really like to know what it was." This mattered so much and her heart was pounding.

"I'll tell you, honey, but first I have a question." Her father's expression was half tender, half fiercely protective. "How do you feel about him?"

"Mom didn't tell you?" Obviously the female members of the Crawford family could keep things to themselves better than the men. But there was no reason to keep her feelings a secret. On some level they already knew. "I love him, Dad."

"You're sure?"

"Positive," she said.

"Then we screwed up, boys." He glanced at each of his sons.

"Dad was the one who shut the door in his face," Kane said when she looked at him.

"Why would you do that?" she demanded.

"I told him that he wasn't getting past us unless he could convince me that he wouldn't hurt my little girl."

"So he said nothing." Since he couldn't love her, there wasn't anything he could say. The hurt of it smacked her again.

"Not exactly." Her father rubbed his palm over the back of his neck. "He said that he thinks he loves you."

"Really?" Thinking he did was better than being positive he didn't.

"It was great, sis," Kane said. "Dad told him to come back when he was sure and shut the door in his face. You should have seen it."

She wished she had because she could have stopped it. If she had, her heart wouldn't be breaking now. Just to think he loved her was a giant step for Justin. They could have talked about this. Now...

Emma wasn't sure whether to be grateful for the family support or upset that they'd chased off the only man she would ever love. The choice was made when a single tear slid down her cheek.

"Oh, baby...don't cry."

Her father looked as if he would rather cut off his right arm than see her shedding tears. And her brothers were showing a similar tendency.

"He didn't leave that long ago," Zach said. "I'll go get him."

"I'm coming, too," Pierce chimed in.

"They might need help. Three is better than one. Don't worry, sis. We'll bring him back so you can talk to him," Kane assured her.

She shook her head. "If he discouraged so easily, there's not really anything to say—"

A sudden knock on the door beside them startled everyone and they froze. Emma recovered first because she had a pretty good idea who was there.

"I'll get it," she said.

"Let me handle this." Alan was closer and blocked the way as he opened the door.

Emma couldn't see over her father's shoulder but recognized Justin's voice.

"Alan— Mr. Crawford— Sir," he said. "I'm not leaving until you let me see her."

"Okay, son."

When her father stepped aside, she was face-to-face with Justin. She heard footsteps on the stairs and her mother's voice asking what was going on. All the Crawfords were present and accounted for.

Then Emma tuned them out and focused on Justin. "Hi."

He started to reach for her then let his hand fall to his side. "Emma—"

She studied his handsome face, the tired gray eyes and haggard expression. "You look terrible."

"That's what Camille said." One corner of his mouth curved up. "She and Ben are watching Kyle. Just so you know."

"How is he?"

"He misses you."

"I miss him, too." Moisture blurred her eyes again, but this time she battled it back, refusing to let him see. "Why are you here?"

Justin looked at the men behind her and pressed his lips tightly together. "To bring you home."

Nothing about loving her. "Why should I believe you're not just trying to keep your nanny?"

"I'm not a liar like the man who cheated on you." He moved close enough for her to feel the heat from his body. "But it was a lie of omission when I used the wrong L-word. The truth is that I don't just want you in my life, I want to make a life with you. I want more children with you. To spend holidays together."

"He looks sincere," Kane said behind her. Someone that sounded like her mother shushed him. "Just saying maybe you should cut him some slack."

"I don't deserve it," he said. "But if you do agree to come back, this probably won't be the last time we hit a speed bump. I don't understand why, but I want that, too. I want to laugh and fight and make up." He was looking at her father, his expression saying exactly how he planned on making up and didn't care what any of them thought about that.

"Pretend they aren't there," she told him.

"Kind of hard." His expression turned wry. "But I don't care who hears. I drew a line in the sand because I was afraid to cross it and get personal. It was a stupid stand to take. My only excuse is that I was attracted to you from the first time I saw you. And I started falling for you when I could see how much you cared about your family. You were more worried about what was best for them than you were for yourself. I've never met a more beautiful, self-less woman."

"Is anyone writing this stuff down?" Pierce asked and was shushed by his mother.

"I'm in love with you," Justin said, then nodded at her father. "I don't think it. I'm absolutely certain. Give me a chance to ask you to marry me. I swear it will be a proper proposal and I'll do it right this time."

"For goodness' sake, Emma—" That was her mother's voice. "Say yes and put the poor man out of his misery."

"Not unless you love me," he cautioned.

"I feel as if I've said it to everyone *except* the man who matters most." She threw herself into his arms. "I love you so much, Justin. More than anything, I want to marry you. There's no need to ask again because what you just said felt so incredibly right. It was truth straight from your heart. Being with you and Kyle feels right, too. I love that little boy as if he were my own. I want to be a mother to him."

"I know you do." He buried his face in her hair. "Thank God I didn't mess this up."

The sound of applause, shrill whistling and very loud cheering made her smile. "I think that means you don't have to ask my father for permission."

"That's a relief. He drives a hard bargain." There was laughter in his voice. "I might have to give up my first-born for his little girl."

"Take good care of her, son."

"Yes, sir. I plan to." Then he looked into her eyes. "I know you've just started to get used to the last name Craw-ford, but if it's okay with you and your family, I'd like to change it to Flint as soon as possible."

"That works for me." She glanced over her shoulder and saw her mother, father and three brothers alternately nod-ding and giving thumbs-up. She'd missed so much with them but was incredibly thankful that her family was there to see the beginning of the rest of her life with the man she loved. "Looks like it's unanimous."

Emma snuggled into Justin and smiled. She'd come to Blackwater Lake looking for her family, but it never crossed her mind that she would find the man of her dreams, too.

Now she had it all—family and forever.

* * * * *

COMING NEXT MONTH FROM

H HARLEQUIN®

SPECIAL EDITION

Available March 20, 2014

#2323 A HOUSE FULL OF FORTUNES!
The Fortunes of Texas: Welcome to Horseback Hollow
by Judy Duarte

Toby Fortune Jones knows his purpose in life. He's a cowboy and foster dad to three adorable kids. But Angie Edwards is still drifting—until she meets Toby. Suddenly, Angie gets swept up into a life she's always dreamed of...but is she ready, willing and able to make a family with the fetching Fortune?

#2324 MORE THAN SHE EXPECTED
Jersey Boys • by Karen Templeton

Tyler Noble's happily-ever-after involves nothing more than his salvage business and his rescue dog. When pregnant beauty Laurel Kent moves in next door, however, troubled Tyler finds his outlook on life slowly changing. Can "Mr. Right Now" leave his past behind to create a forever family with Laurel?

#2325 A CAMDEN FAMILY WEDDING
The Camdens of Colorado • by Victoria Pade

Dane Camden is only interested in working on his grandmother's happily-ever-after...until he meets Vonni Hunter. Eager to settle down—but not with bachelor Dane—Vonni's hesitant about taking a job planning the Camden matriarch's nuptials. But she can't deny her attraction to the hunky Camden as she realizes domestic bliss might just be closer than she thinks.

#2326 ONE NIGHT WITH THE BOSS
The Bachelors of Blackwater Lake • by Teresa Southwick

Olivia Lawson wants her boss, Brady O'Keefe, more than any raise. Brady's seemingly oblivious to her feelings, so Olivia decides to move away and start a new life. When the boss demands a reason for her departure, Olivia invents a fake boyfriend. But Brady's not buying her fib—or the sudden turn of events that might take his gorgeous assistant away forever....

#2327 CELEBRATION'S BABY
Celebrations, Inc. • by Nancy Robards Thompson

When a one-night affair leaves journalist Bia Anderson pregnant, her best friend, Aiden Woods, steps up as her child's "father"—and her fiancé. Little does Bia know, though, that Aiden's been in love with her for years, but has never acted on it. As they bond over her unborn baby, a friendship turns into the love of a lifetime.

#2328 RECIPE FOR ROMANCE • by Olivia Miles

Baker Emily Porter is shocked when her long-lost love, Scott Collins, comes back to town. Scott's got an unwelcome secret—and it's not just that he's still madly in love with Emily. Tension rises as sparks fly between the ex-lovers, but will long-buried lies destroy their relationship?

YOU CAN FIND MORE INFORMATION ON UPCOMING HARLEQUIN® TITLES, FREE EXCERPTS AND MORE AT WWW.HARLEQUIN.COM.

HSECNM0314

REQUEST YOUR FREE BOOKS!

2 FREE NOVELS PLUS 2 FREE GIFTS!

⬧ HARLEQUIN

SPECIAL EDITION

Life, Love & Family

YES! Please send me 2 FREE Harlequin® Special Edition novels and my 2 FREE gifts (gifts are worth about $10). After receiving them, if I don't wish to receive any more books, I can return the shipping statement marked "cancel." If I don't cancel, I will receive 6 brand-new novels every month and be billed just $4.74 per book in the U.S. or $5.24 per book in Canada. That's a savings of at least 14% off the cover price! It's quite a bargain! Shipping and handling is just 50¢ per book in the U.S. and 75¢ per book in Canada.* I understand that accepting the 2 free books and gifts places me under no obligation to buy anything. I can always return a shipment and cancel at any time. Even if I never buy another book, the two free books and gifts are mine to keep forever.

235/335 HDN F45Y

Name	(PLEASE PRINT)

Address	Apt. #

City	State/Prov.	Zip/Postal Code

Signature (if under 18, a parent or guardian must sign)

Mail to the Harlequin® Reader Service:
IN U.S.A.: P.O. Box 1867, Buffalo, NY 14240-1867
IN CANADA: P.O. Box 609, Fort Erie, Ontario L2A 5X3

Want to try two free books from another line?
Call 1-800-873-8635 or visit www.ReaderService.com.

* Terms and prices subject to change without notice. Prices do not include applicable taxes. Sales tax applicable in N.Y. Canadian residents will be charged applicable taxes. Offer not valid in Quebec. This offer is limited to one order per household. Not valid for current subscribers to Harlequin Special Edition books. All orders subject to credit approval. Credit or debit balances in a customer's account(s) may be offset by any other outstanding balance owed by or to the customer. Please allow 4 to 6 weeks for delivery. Offer available while quantities last.

Your Privacy—The Harlequin® Reader Service is committed to protecting your privacy. Our Privacy Policy is available online at www.ReaderService.com or upon request from the Harlequin Reader Service.

We make a portion of our mailing list available to reputable third parties that offer products we believe may interest you. If you prefer that we not exchange your name with third parties, or if you wish to clarify or modify your communication preferences, please visit us at www.ReaderService.com/consumerschoice or write to us at Harlequin Reader Service Preference Service, P.O. Box 9062, Buffalo, NY 14269. Include your complete name and address.

HSE13R

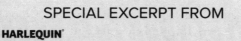
Olivia Lawson is hopelessly—and unrequitedly—in love with her gorgeous boss, Brady O'Keefe. To get over him, the lovely assistant decides to move away from Blackwater Lake—and invents a fake boyfriend as an excuse. But Brady's starting to realize he doesn't want the beautiful redhead out of his life....

***

"If you didn't meet him on vacation, it must have been a trip for work," said Brady.

"Remind me not to try and put anything over on you."

Sarcasm was one of his favorite things about her. "So, was it in Austin? Seattle? Atlanta?"

"I definitely went to those cities. You should know. We were there together."

She was right about that, but when business hours were over they'd gone their separate ways. If Olivia had met men, she'd never said anything to him. Until now.

As crazy as he knew it was, he wanted to know everything. "Do you have a job lined up in Leonard's neck of the woods?"

"I have an offer."

"I'd be happy to give you a glowing recommendation."

She stood and walked to the doorway of his office. "Any other questions?"

Why are you leaving me?

Brady didn't say that out loud, even though the idea of it

had preoccupied him way too much since she'd dropped her bombshell. Besides his mother, sister and niece, he had no personal attachments—yet somehow he'd become attached to Olivia. He wouldn't be making that mistake with his next assistant.

She looked over her shoulder on the way out the door. "I'll be lining up more candidates to interview. And if you know what's good for you, you'll approach this process more seriously than you just did."

"I conducted those interviews very seriously."

She ignored that. "You need to ask yourself what's wrong with the two women you saw today."

"I don't need to ask myself anything. I already know what's wrong."

"Care to share?" She put a hand on her hip.

"Neither of them is you."

***

Enjoy this sneak peek from Teresa Southwick's
ONE NIGHT WITH THE BOSS,
the latest installment in her
Harlequin® Special Edition miniseries
THE BACHELORS OF BLACKWATER LAKE,
on sale in April 2014!